Praise for Beth Williamson's The Treasure

5 Bl⋯⋯⋯ ⋯ ⋯⋯ book in the Malloys Family series and if you have not read any of these books by now you are definitely missing out. If you like your hero's hot, hard and packing and your heroines smart, sassy and not afraid to go after what they want than you will love this series. While THE TREASURE can definitely stand alone, I guarantee once you read it you will be running to grab up the rest of the stories in this awesome series. Congratulations Mrs. Williamson on another wonderful story." ~ *Dina Smith, Romance Junkies*

4 Cups "...Absolutely Delightful! Ms. Williamson has penned another exciting historical that is wonderfully entertaining, and exceptionally told. Exceptional characters and very important secondary characters are the key to this amazing tale. Exploding with adventure and engaging dialogue this story packs a punch. Add steamy love scenes and you have a story you will want to read over and over again. I know this reader is looking forward to the next Malloy story." ~ *Wateena, Coffee Time Romance*

"Beth Williamson's latest Malloy family story gives us a heroine who is a sweet little spitfire with enough love and kindness in her to fill an entire town...As expected, whenever I read a Beth Williamson story it is well written, hilarious, but also heart wrenching. Nothing to date has come easy for this loving family that once you're a part of there's nothing they won't do for you.!" ~ Rachelle, *Fallen Angel Reviews*

"The Treasure by Beth Williamson struck me right in the gut. ...The Treasure was by far the most touching and heart wrenching novel I have read from Ms. Williamson. ...Ms. Williamson continues to bring to life this wonderful family and I anxiously await the continuation of this series!" ~ *Talia Ricci, Joyfully Reviewed*

THE TREASURE

Beth Williamson

A Samhain Publishing, Ltd. publication.

Samhain Publishing, Ltd.
2932 Ross Clark Circle, #384
Dothan, AL 36301
www.samhainpublishing.com

The Treasure
Copyright © 2006 by Beth Williamson
Print ISBN: 1-59998-274-9
Digital ISBN: 1-59998-050-9

Editing by Sasha Knight
Cover by Scott Carpenter

First Samhain Publishing, Ltd. electronic publication: July 2006
First Samhain Publishing, Ltd. print publication: October 2006

DEDICATION

For my husband who accepts me, a clumsy blunder puss, as I am. Here's to all the klutzes and the men who love them.

CHAPTER ONE

New York, New York, January 1889

Lillian Wickham knew she was clumsy. No use hiding behind fancy words like "accident prone" to cushion the blow. Living at St. Catherine's, she'd had so many cuts, bruises, scrapes, broken bones and sprained joints the infirmary had a box full of supplies just for her. She'd fallen, tripped up and down stairs, gotten thrown from a carriage, had a foot run over by a flower cart, and banged her head all the time. The plain truth was she didn't have enough grace to fill a thimble.

Lily was sure God had given her enough optimism and enthusiasm to make up for being such a blunder puss. She always tried to see the bright side of every misfortune and kept her optimism around her like a shield. The nuns at the orphanage would roll their eyes and pick her up from wherever she'd fallen, check for blood, then send her on her way. She struggled so hard not to make mistakes and the more she worked at it, the more spectacular the mistakes.

There was the time she accidentally set the kitchen on fire making her first batch of biscuits. Or when she'd ruined at least ten of the nuns' habits by using the soap she'd invented. And she had just lost a governess position, again. This time for breaking a vase in the Carmichael's home. She hadn't intended to knock it over, but when her cloak got caught in the door, she pulled and pulled. Unfortunately, when the door suddenly opened, she fell backwards…right into the vase. Apparently from the Ming dynasty in China, too. They hadn't made her pay for it, thank the Lord, but they had dismissed her without paying her last two weeks wages. This was the eighth time in as many years she had lost her job because of her problem. At twenty-six, she could not afford to lose her wages or her job anymore.

Lily sighed and continued unpacking her clothes from the valise and hanging them on the hooks on the wall. She was lucky the orphanage needed a temporary teacher while Sister Mary Agnes was on sabbatical for a month. She had to find another position and fast. There was no way she would be a charity case again.

"Lily?"

She turned to see the Reverend Mother in the doorway to her room. The nuns called them cells, but she just couldn't bring herself to do that. Life could be dreary enough without thinking of your living quarters as a cell. The Reverend Mother had been like a mother to her, as well as a confidante, advisor and friend. Lily had never asked the older woman's age, but with her wrinkled face she must be at least sixty if not older. Her eyes, however, remained a vibrant, sparkling blue.

"Hello, Reverend Mother. I just want to say again how grateful I am."

She held up her hand and stopped Lily's gratitude. "No need, child. We had an opening and you needed it. It's the Lord's way of keeping the wheel of life turning."

The older woman came in and sat on the edge of the bed.

"I have heard of a position you might be interested in."

Lily stopped what she was doing and sat beside her. "Really? Oh, that's wonderful."

"Before you get yourself too excited, let me tell you what it entails."

"Absolutely."

Lily hoped it was in Manhattan. She loved the tall buildings and being able to walk in Central Park, not to mention the museums and restaurants.

"I have a friend who I've known all my life. She and I grew up together and have kept in touch for years."

"How lovely for you. I hope you and I will still write after so long."

"Yes, child, now hush up a minute and let me finish." The Reverend Mother raised one silver eyebrow.

"Sorry," Lily mumbled and put an invisible button on her lips. Another one of her flaws. She talked too much.

"Francesca and her husband own a ranch in Wyoming. They have six children. The oldest, Raymond, has a five-year-old daughter, with no wife, and is in desperate need of a housekeeper and governess for the child. The pay is not much, fifty dollars a month, but it includes room and board and a clothing allowance."

Lily held her breath until she felt dizzy. *Wyoming?* That was out in the west, where things were…wild. Certainly nothing like New York, a place Lily considered home after so much traveling when she was a child.

"They are good people, Lily. And this is an opportunity for you to start over. Where people don't gossip about how much trouble you are as a governess when you start breaking things or falling down the stairs."

"That only happened once." Lily felt her cheeks pinken at the memory.

The Reverend Mother waved her hand again. "I know, but the more people gossip, the harder it is for you to find a permanent position. Who knows, you may even find you like it out West and find a young man to marry."

Lily laughed. "Only if he doesn't mind his wife being the clumsiest person on earth."

The Reverend Mother cupped Lily's cheek and smiled, her warm brown eyes sympathetic. "Do not be so hard on yourself, Lily. You are a wonderful person. Any man would be happy and proud to have you as his bride."

Lily blushed and stared down at her hands. "It's so far away, Mother, and I don't know anything about Wyoming. I would miss you and it's…out West."

"Yes, it is. You don't have much time to decide, less than two months. After that, you must be on a train bound for Wyoming or find another position here in New York. And neither choice will be easy."

She stood and touched Lily on the head as she had done countless times.

"Think about it. It could be a whole new beginning for you."

After she left the room, Lily stared out the small window above her narrow bed.

Wyoming? What did she know about Wyoming?

ℭℜ ℬℴ

Exactly eight weeks later, Lily stood on the platform at Grand Central Railroad Station and clutched her battered valise in one hand. Her heart pounded, her mouth was as dry as cotton, and a trickle of perspiration snaked down her spine.

She was nervous. She had read all she could about Wyoming, and even corresponded with Mr. Raymond Malloy. He was polite and factual. She could not tell anything about him as a person from his letter. He described his daughter as "difficult" and "in need of a woman's firm hand and a thorough education" but otherwise gave no details about either one of them.

The soles on her boots were almost worn through, so she would need to purchase new shoes. She hoped Mr. Malloy would advance her some of the clothing allowance. The sisters had purchased a navy wool coat for her, and Sister Mary Francis had knitted her warm mittens and a hat. They were all such wonderful people. Without them, she would not be the person she was now. Each of them were her teachers growing up and taught her how to love, learn, and how to accept what she could not change and fight for what she could.

Lily's journey would pass through a good deal of America. Since she hadn't been beyond the borders of New York in more than ten years, she was excited to see what had changed. The conductor shouted "All aboard" and she nodded at the train like a ninny, as if accepting the challenge. In a way she was, and so she strode toward the train and stepped up inside.

Lily Wickham was on her way to Wyoming.

CHAPTER TWO

Cheshire, Wyoming, March, 1889

Ray Malloy was nervous. It was cold as a bitch that morning and his damn palms were sweaty in his gloves. Couldn't feel his fingers after driving the wagon to the train station in freezing temperatures, but his goddamned, nervous palms were clammy.

He didn't know what to expect from Miss Wickham. She sounded pretty proper and very smart in her letter. There wasn't any personal information exchanged other than their names. He regretted that now. He could have at least asked how old she was, but hell, Mama said she lived with the nuns.

Truth was he didn't know much about nuns. Or about Miss Lillian Wickham. He hoped she wasn't a nasty old troll with a hairy wart and a stooped back.

He didn't trust his instincts with women. After all, he had gotten trapped in the web of the most conniving, innocent-looking black widow spider in the whole Wyoming territory. His wife. Ex-wife now. Regina had skipped town a month after their daughter, Melody, was born. She divorced him six months later from San Francisco.

He hadn't been with a woman since. Self-imposed celibacy was something he would have in common with Miss Wickham. Five years was a long time, but he didn't trust women, excluding his sister, sisters-in-law and mother, of course. Unfortunately, aside from his family, Melody didn't have any contact with other children or women.

And, he thought with a grimace, it definitely showed. She was nearly impossible to track, had a mouth like a sailor, and absolutely refused to wear "girlie" clothes or even take a bath more than once a month. She was a handful. Make that two handfuls. He had no idea how to raise her. He was obviously doing a shitty job of it, judging by the wildness.

Ray prayed Miss Wickham would be able to do something with Melody. She needed to learn her reading and writing, and maybe some ciphering. And she sure as hell needed to learn manners beyond asking "Where's the biscuits, Pa?".

He loved Melody fiercely and hoped he hadn't caused too much damage to her by his ways. Ray knew he wasn't affectionate, or patient, or even friendly most of the time. Melody was a tiny version of him, down to the scowl she wore when she was angry. His heart ached with the need to do right by her. Against his better judgment, he'd listened to his mother and hired the damn governess, a fancy word for teacher. Truth be told, he hadn't been able to find someone willing to teach Melody in the entire state of Wyoming. That left him standing on the Cheshire train platform with clammy hands and a twisted-up gut.

Ray shuffled his feet on the wood-planked floor, trying to get the circulation going to his toes. In the distance, the train whistle shrieked, and inside, he jumped a country mile.

Miss Wickham was about to arrive.

ℭℜ ℘

As Lily stepped from the train at the Cheshire station and set her valise down, she began to search the people on the platform for her new employer. She had bid goodbye to New York nearly a week ago, and here she was finally in Wyoming. It seemed like a dream, like it was happening to someone else. As she had crossed over the great country, she kept a journal of everything she saw. From rivers, to beautiful buildings, buffalo, wild horses and everything in between. It was all incredible and each amazing sight made her decision the best one she had ever made. Without it, she would never have seen all the treasures she'd been too busy to see when she was a child.

The first thing she noticed about Wyoming was it was really cold. Not the kind of cold on the streets of New York. But a biting, gnawing cold that chewed at her cheeks and left them numb. There was snow everywhere she looked. Even on the roof of the train depot. And icicles hung down, some of them at least a foot long. It was a winter wonderland. She pinched herself to stop gawking and started searching for Mr. Malloy again.

After the steam from the locomotive's engines cleared, she saw a man standing alone in the middle of the platform.

Now that was a *big* man.

Squaring her shoulders, as well as her resolve, she picked up her valise and headed towards him.

"Mr. Malloy?" she asked when she was about ten feet away.

As she approached him, he took off his hat and regarded her with a bruising stare. He nodded at her question as his large hands tightened perceptibly on his hat. Setting her valise down, she straightened herself up to her full height of not quite five feet. His wavy hair was varying shades of brown and red, and his eyes were a deep emerald green. Yes, indeed, he was quite an imposing size. His bold gaze raked her up and down without a flicker of warmth. She shivered and wasn't at all sure it was from the frigidly cold air.

"This isn't going to work, Miss Wickham. I was expecting an older woman. Why, you're no bigger than a minute, probably not even eighteen yet. Wyoming is no place for a woman like you. Go back to New York." He turned, leaving her standing on the train platform.

Well, we'll see about that.

"Mr. Malloy," she said loudly as she reached out to grab his arm. He stopped short and stared down at her hand as if it were an offensive creature biting him.

"Don't touch me." His voice was low, but incredibly forceful.

The fierceness of his command was not lost on Lily. She removed her hand promptly, but with dignity nonetheless.

"My apologies." She took a deep breath. "I assure you, Mr. Malloy, I am not a child. I am a twenty-six-year-old woman, long since put on the shelf. As I wrote in my letter, I have served as a governess and tutor for eight years for many of the finest families in New York. Mother Superior has corresponded with your mother about me and gave me a sterling recommendation. I am strong, capable and intelligent. I will not be turned away like a beggar looking for food. You offered me a position, sir, and I took you at your word. I always keep mine." She finished with a firm nod, a trick she'd long ago learned when dealing with recalcitrant children. Thank God he hadn't noticed her knees knocking together so hard, they almost sounded like drums.

His right eyebrow rose as she spoke. "Think highly of yourself then?"

She knew her cheeks looked like crimson banners, but she refused to back down. This was her future they were talking about, not a parlor conversation about fashion.

"No, I'm simply stating the facts. I am well qualified for the position you offered as your daughter's tutor, and I'm a more than adequate housekeeper. More than that, I…I need the position. I have nothing to go back to in New York, and no funds to get there." She hated to admit it to this man, but the trip to Wyoming cost her nearly every cent she owned. She was, to put it bluntly, poor as a church mouse.

He studied her with his razor-sharp gaze for a minute before sighing long and hard.

"Wyoming isn't a forgiving place, Miss Wickham, and I'm not a forgiving man. We're both hard, cold and demand respect. I don't accept excuses from the people who work for me. The first time one of my hands endangers anyone, or lies to me, they're out on their ass. Do I make myself clear?"

"Perfectly. Does this mean I'm hired?" Her heart began to beat a staccato rhythm as hope burned in her chest.

"Temporarily, but only until you've earned enough to return to New York. Don't try to convince me otherwise, because my mind is made up."

With that, he picked up her valise and started walking at a brisk pace down the platform.

Good heavens, the man has legs a mile long.

Lily had to nearly break into a run to keep up with him. As he rounded the corner, he stopped to speak to someone. Unfortunately, as quickly as she was walking, Lily had no time to slow down. She glimpsed dark hair and blue eyes of another man before plowing into Mr. Malloy with all the grace of a toddler learning to walk. She tilted backwards, then landed square on her backside on the hard planks. Her teeth clamped together painfully and she bit her tongue.

"Are you all right?" the stranger asked as he reached out a hand to help her stand.

"Yes, I'm fine. How clumsy of me." She hoped like blazes her cheeks were not as red as they felt. That was not the first impression she hoped to make. As she surreptitiously brushed off her behind, she watched the men's reactions.

The stranger turned and scowled at Mr. Malloy. "It wasn't your fault, ma'am. My big brother here seems to have forgotten his manners and was plowing along without you."

Big brother? Yes, that would explain the resemblance. They were both tall and broad-shouldered with similar features.

"Shut up, Jack," growled Mr. Malloy. "Mind your own business. What the hell are you doing here anyway?"

"You're not giving your governess a good impression here, Ray. Becky asked me to come down and make sure you were ah…I mean, to lend a hand."

The stranger held out his hand for her to shake. "Jack Malloy. Welcome to Wyoming, Miss Wickham."

As she gratefully shook the proffered hand, her small, gloved one was nearly swallowed by his, yet all he did was give her a gentle squeeze.

"Lily Wickham. Thank you for your welcome, Mr. Malloy."

She did not look at her employer when she spoke, but she saw his scowl deepen out of the corner of her eye.

"Call me Jack."

His blue eyes were as warm as his smile. She was definitely going to like him.

"Of course, as long as you call me Lily."

"Do you have any other bags you need to be fetched?" He eyed her threadbare valise with a doubtful look.

"Yes, I have a trunk out on the platform."

"I'll be back in two shakes." He walked back toward the station, leaving Lily alone with her new employer.

Lily finally turned her gaze to Mr. Malloy. His face was like a thundercloud, dark and stormy.

"How far is it to your ranch, Mr. Malloy?"

He hesitated, then yanked off his hat and slapped his thigh with it. Slamming it back on his head, he pursed his lips and looked up.

"It's about an hour." He let out a breath through clenched teeth. "Why don't you...uh...call me Ray?"

Lily blinked and then smiled her friendliest grin. "That's very kind of you. Most employers don't allow their governesses to address them so casually. Being in the West is much more informal. I would be honored to call you Ray. Please call me Lily."

He nodded once, grabbed her valise and stalked toward the steps leading to the street. A wagon waited there with two large brown horses attached. Another horse was tied to a hitching post beside the wagon.

Ray dropped her valise into the back, walked to the horses and ran his hands up and down their noses, speaking softly to them.

He obviously wasn't a bad man, but his first impression needed a bit of work. If she wasn't so desperate for a job, for a new beginning, she would consider getting on the next eastbound train. This position was not going to be easy if the father was any indication of the child's temperament.

It might just turn out to be the hardest job of her life.

CR SO

Ray still couldn't believe his eyes. He tried to calm his racing heart.

Holy shit.

He hadn't expected her to look like she had stepped out of a Renaissance painting.

In a word, Lily Wickham was luscious. Curvy, round, soft, she had lips that could give a man erotic dreams for years. She resembled a tiny goddess and had an air of sensuality that made his blood thrum. Her simple wool coat certainly wasn't unseemly, but it hugged her hourglass figure like a lover. She had a natural sway to her walk that surely made most men sit up and take notice. He couldn't see her hair color beneath the bonnet she wore, but it wouldn't make his first impression any different. She was trouble in a small, curvy package and his internal warning bells were clanging up a storm. There was no question—he had to send her back to New York. He couldn't live in a house with her in it, even with his vow to never marry again. Surely a small ranch in Wyoming wouldn't keep a woman who looked like that entertained for very long.

When Ray had felt her warm, soft body slam into his with breasts that seemed overly large for such a tiny woman, for a moment, a flickering moment, he remembered what it felt like to hold a woman. He had the crazy notion to lie on top of her and rub his hardness against her softness as she lay sprawled on the platform. He still had a hard-on for God's sake! From looking at a woman and two seconds of those soft, pillowy breasts pushing against his back. He shuddered from the memory and tried to command his cock to stop bellowing.

Ray slowly breathed in and out for a few minutes while waiting for Jack and Lily.

Lily. Even the name conjured up carnal thoughts. He needed to find a way to send her back without looking like he was running scared. And he wasn't, dammit. There wasn't a thing about Lily that scared him.

If he kept telling himself that lie, perhaps he'd believe it eventually.

CR ℘

Jack came back with her trunk in his hands and a smile on his face.

"This is heavy. Do you collect books?"

She nodded. "When I can. Most of those are from a teacher of mine who gifted them to me when I became a governess."

He whistled. "Nice gift. You must have meant a lot to her."

Lily smiled. "She certainly meant a lot to me." She bit her lip to concentrate on the here and now, and not the past that hovered. The past that called to her to remember her sins. Of pride. Of selfishness. She shook off the demon riding her shoulder and slapped it aside. Now was not the time to wallow.

She followed Jack down the stairs, wishing desperately not to fall, trip or bump into him. That would certainly go well after her ignominious fall five minutes earlier. Ray would look at her askance if she couldn't keep her own two feet on the ground, much less his daughter's.

"His bark is worse than his bite," Jack said under his breath. "Don't think too badly of him. He's had a real rough time of it."

"I don't think badly of him, Jack. I wanted, or rather, I hoped we could at least be friends." Which was true. She always wanted a friendly relationship with her employers. It just seemed something went wrong to ruin that relationship, each and every time. This time was obviously no different. Mr. Malloy wasn't a happy man to begin with, and the inauspicious beginning to their relationship didn't help matters any.

Jack started down the steps with his burden and waited for Lily to keep up with him. As she followed carefully behind him, she kept her gaze locked on Ray.

"Ray doesn't have any friends." He shook his head. "Maybe you can be the first."

"What on earth happened to him?" She realized she had voiced the words aloud. Her cheeks colored again. Dang her runaway tongue.

"Not my place to tell you," Jack said simply.

He set her heavy trunk in the wagon with a thump, then turned to help Lily climb to the seat next to Ray, but she had already scrambled up there. Jack tipped his head and smiled.

"Nice to have met you, Lily. Good luck."

"Thank you, Jack. Do you visit the ranch often?"

Before Jack could form a reply, Ray slapped the reins on the horses' rumps and the wagon lurched forward. Lily reached out to grab Ray's arm to steady herself, and he hissed at her. After dropping his arm like a hot rock, she found purchase on the wagon seat as they headed down the somewhat frozen, muddy street.

"Goodbye, Jack," she called over her shoulder. She wanted to lecture her new employer about his atrocious manners, but she didn't want him to turn the wagon around and drop her back at the train platform. Her bottom was already quite sore from riding on the train for so long, and her clumsy fall certainly didn't help matters any. And now, here she was, bouncing on a hard wagon bench with no cushion whatsoever. She hoped Mr. Malloy's ranch had a nice tub, because she couldn't think of anything more enticing than a warm bath.

"Don't go looking at Jack as a good marriage prospect. He's already married, happily, too, with three kids," he growled at her. "I don't need one of my employees to get cow-eyed over my little brother."

"Cow-eyed?" Lily was incredulous. "I'll do nothing of the sort, Mr. Malloy. Your brother is a nice man, and I was being polite to him. There isn't more, nor will there ever be, to my relationship with your brother, or any other man for that matter."

"Just so we're clear on it, Miss Wickham."

"Crystal clear, Mr. Malloy."

It was an unpleasant, and decidedly uncomfortable, ride out to the Double R Ranch.

ೞ ೲ

Ray didn't know what to say to her, how to make conversation, so he stayed silent. They bounced along the frozen ground headed for his ranch. He could not even begin to explain how he ended up offering her a job when he hadn't intended on it. She was too...*much*. Deep down, his demons screamed and clawed at him. Taunting him with thoughts of what Miss Wickham looked like under her little wool coat.

With tremendous effort, he beat them back. Life was already a living hell without getting a hard-on every time he looked at Melody's governess. He had a feeling he'd just made one of the biggest decisions in his life. He hoped it was the right one.

Most of the others he'd made turned out wrong.

ೞ ೲ

They finally arrived at their destination after an hour of riding in the bouncy wagon. He stopped in front of a lovely two-story log house set amidst some buildings. She assumed they were all part of the ranch—a barn, or bunkhouse, or something of that nature. The house itself had a long wrap-around porch and two rocking chairs out front.

Ray dismounted with a feline grace that belied his size and went to the back of the wagon to retrieve her valise. As she slowly let herself down to the ground, Lily was embarrassed to realize she wasn't sure she could stand on her own two legs, which at the moment were not only incredibly sore, but also chilled to the bone. However, she wasn't about to let Mr. Malloy know that. He'd think she was too delicate to live in Wyoming. Gripping the side of the wagon, Lily pretended to be looking for something on the floor near the wagon bench while she silently willed her legs to regain their strength.

"Lose something?" He stepped up behind her and his very presence made her body clench.

"Yes, I believe I may have lost a hairpin. Won't take but a moment to find. Don't worry about me; go on inside where it's warm. I'll be right along."

She could practically feel him scowling at her. Ray didn't move a muscle. "Since you're wearing a bonnet, and didn't touch your hair once during the past hour, I can't imagine why you think you lost a hairpin. Even if you did, it would have bounced out of the wagon by now. What are you really doing?"

He was too shrewd, and much too observant. She, of course, was just as shrewd.

"Just because I wasn't touching my hair doesn't mean I can't feel a hairpin missing, Ray."

"Let's go, Lily."

"Fine, then, I'll look later." She let go of the wagon and spun on her right foot to walk. Unfortunately, her legs truly couldn't support her. As she crumpled toward the ground, Ray's arm came around her like a steel band, preventing her fall. All the air whooshed out of her lungs as Ray's arm squeezed her midriff.

Oh, bother it. She'd done it again. Miss Clumsy Trueheart.

Ray helped her stand and quickly removed his arm. "Are you always this graceful?"

"Unfortunately, yes."

He heaved out a frustrated sigh and motioned for her to precede him to the door.

"I can't wait to meet Melody." With a bright tone in her voice, she desperately tried to change the subject.

He mumbled something under his breath that sounded like, "Yeah, if we can find her."

They stepped into the house, which was very poorly lit by a lantern somewhere to her right. In the semi-darkness, it was hard to get a good look at her new home. Lily squinted as they passed through the parlor. Why, that looked like a piano. She had no time to discover the truth as her employer rushed her through the house. Ray pointed in the direction of another darkened room as he continued ceaselessly.

"Kitchen."

He pointed down the hallway. "My room and Melody's room."

Opening a doorway, he gestured for her to enter. "Your room."

He dropped her valise on the floor with a bang, then lit a lamp and set it on the bedside table.

"Make yourself at home. I've got to go unhitch the team."

With that, he left her alone in the cold room. Lily was nearly speechless by Ray's complete lack of civility.

"Well. I guess that's that." She rubbed her arms. "First thing I have to do is get a fire going." She removed her bonnet and coat. Spying a bucket of kindling, she laid a fire in the stone fireplace. Truth be told, she was surprised to see a fireplace in a guest room. After getting a cheery blaze going, she stood to survey the room. It was spacious and open with a double bed in the middle covered with an exquisite wedding-ring quilt. There was a sitting chair and a reading table in the corner, and a colorful rag rug on the floor by the bed. It was too large to be a guestroom. In fact, it looked like the master bedroom.

"Good heavens, I think he's given me his room."

But, no, he clearly said his room was down the hall somewhere.

"Very curious."

"Are you talkin' to somebody?" came a small voice from the darkened hallway.

Lily spun around to try to locate the child in the gloom, but all she saw was a small shadow. It must be Melody, Ray's daughter and her new charge.

"No, just to myself. Sometimes I find that I need to voice my thoughts out loud to help me make up my mind."

"Who are you?"

"I am Miss Lily Wickham. And who are you?"

"Mel."

"It's a pleasure to meet you, Mel. Could I impose on you for a small favor?"

"What favor?"

Lily cleared her throat and straightened her shoulders. "I have just arrived, and I truly need to find the privy. Do you think you can help me?"

The small shadow walked into the room and Lily caught her breath as the child was revealed to her in the firelight. She was filthy, barefoot, wearing worn, oversized boy's pants held up with a rope, and what was on her head looked more like a black rat's nest than hair.

"Ya gotta piss?" She scratched her hair with one grimy hand.

"Well, I do need to take care of some personal business."

"Does that mean yes?"

Lily bit back a grin. Melody was very precocious. "Yes. I would be very grateful if you could point me in the right direction."

Ray Malloy suddenly filled the doorway behind little Mel with Lily's trunk perched on his large shoulder. How did he ever manage to get it up there?

"Mel, scoot out of the way." His voice was almost gentle with his daughter.

Melody moved with the agility of a cat and landed on the reading chair in the corner.

"She's gotta piss, Papa, and can't find the privy." She snickered.

Lily wanted the ground to open up right then and there and swallow her whole. Her entire body flushed bright red from her toes to her hair. What a thing for the child to say in front of her father.

Ray dropped the trunk at the foot of bed with unqualified ease and straightened, his hands fisted on his hips. He quirked an eyebrow at Lily. "That so?"

Lily smiled nervously.

"Show her where it is, Mel. Then bring her to the kitchen so she can get started on supper."

With a final, unreadable glance at his small daughter, Ray left the room.

Trying to calm her nervousness, Lily took two deep, steadying breaths, then turned. Mel had disappeared. Gone like a puff of smoke without a sound. And Lily had no idea where to find the privy to relieve her aching bladder, and no one to ask. From somewhere in the house, Lily heard a small, self-satisfied giggle. What a welcome.

CHAPTER THREE

After fifteen minutes of searching outside, Lily gratefully found the privy. It was in the house the whole time. It had very modern indoor plumbing, with a large claw-footed tub. The tub was obviously not used since it was covered with a layer of dust, and the child who needed to use it was as dirty as a baby pig. After finally relieving herself, Lily went to the kitchen.

So, Miss Melody Malloy was a little hoyden. Lily could handle it; she was itching for the challenge actually. Being bested in the first round pricked her pride a bit. She should have seen it coming, after all, Melody's father was no mannerly gentleman.

After lighting a fire in the rather new looking, but dusty, black cook stove, Lily set out to review the supplies in the pantry. Like everything she'd seen in the house, it was sorely lacking. There was barely enough supplies to last a few days, and the meals would consist of biscuits and beans with coffee to wash it down. She saw a butter churn in one corner and wondered if her employer had a milking cow. She hadn't milked a cow in years, but she knew it would come back to her quickly. Milk and butter would help the meals nicely, as would some eggs if there were any laying hens.

After putting some beans to soak, Lily decided she needed to make a list of supplies to purchase. Surely Mr. Malloy couldn't begrudge her a stock of food stuffs if she was to be an adequate housekeeper and cook. She retrieved a pencil and paper from her valise and began to make a list. Twenty minutes later, Ray found her sitting at the table, nibbling the end of the pencil.

"Supper 'bout ready?"

His gruff question knocked Lily out of her reverie with a startled yelp.

"Oh! Ray, you scared me. Why, you're as quiet as a cat with socks." She smiled as she stood to check the beans. "I just popped the biscuits in the oven, and the beans should be ready about the same time. About fifteen minutes I'd say. Do you want to find Melody and help her wash up?"

Ray grimaced. "Not even my sister Nicky could make her wash up. She just squirms like a puppy, then runs and hides."

Lily's brows rose in surprise. "Truly?"

Ray's expression told her he expected censure or at least a snide remark after he nodded to her one-word question. She gave him neither.

"I love a challenge. Please keep an eye on the food." Determination beat a tattoo in her. "Miss Melody will be clean for this meal."

She pushed up her sleeves and went in search of her small charge.

ᙓ ᙒ

"Dammit, leggo! I ain't gonna do it."

Ray heard his daughter's curse from his seat on the porch. He had gone outside to sit in the rocking chair, determined not to be involved in the battle of wills raging in house. Miss Wickham was determined Mel would be clean; Mel was determined to remain dirty. Miss Wickham seemed to be winning, although it was not a sure victory.

"I'll let go of you when you're clean with your hair combed properly, and not a moment sooner," came Lily's prim reply.

"Ouch! That hurts, you stupid heifer!"

He really ought to talk to Mel about her language. No little girl should talk like a ranch hand, even if that's all she was around her entire life. Once she was a bit older, maybe he would send her to one of those finishing schools so she could learn to be a lady like Miss Wickham.

"My pa's gonna whoop your ass for this, lady."

Ray lurched to his feet and strode into the house. He'd had enough of listening to the battle. It was time to end the war.

When he stepped into the kitchen, he had to blink twice at the image before him. Melody was wearing clean shirt and trousers, and wonder of wonders, she was free of dirt and grime. Her thick, black hair was combed and braided into two pigtails. Her cheeks were rosy red, and her black eyes were shooting fire.

Miss Wickham, however, was quite wet from the ordeal. So wet her dress clung to her curves like a second skin, and her nipples puckered with the cold. A jolt shot through Ray's body, like somebody poked him with a sharp stick. When his gaze clashed with hers, it seemed she read his thoughts.

She frowned. "I'll just go put on a clean dress. Mr. Malloy, would you please keep Melody company, and clean, for two minutes while I change?"

Without waiting for an answer, she exited the kitchen.

"You look right nice, Mel." He removed his hat and coat, then sat in one of the kitchen chairs.

"I don't wanna look nice, Pa." She stuck out her lower lip. "I hate her."

Every time he looked at his daughter, it reminded him of his past follies, of his wife's betrayal, of the miserable hell his life had become in the past five years. He knew he wasn't doing right by Melody, which was the main reason he decided to hire a housekeeper and governess for her. Folks in town called her "wild thing". Some even called her a bastard since she didn't favor either of her parents. She was, however, the child of his heart regardless of whether or not he was truly her father, and he loved her more than life itself. It cut him to the bone to see the other children, and adults, whisper nasty rumors about his little girl. He hoped Miss Wickham would help Melody become more civilized, more accepted, and in turn, a proper young lady.

"That's not a very nice thing to say."

Melody blushed slightly, but didn't relax her combative stance. "I know that, but Aunt Nicky says sometimes things need saying."

"I don't think she meant being rude to people, Melody."

"Was I rude?"

"Yes, honey, you were. You owe Miss Wickham an apology."

She wrinkled up her nose and scowled. "Don't wanna."

Ray sighed. "The hardest things in life to do are the things that we want to do the least. You will apologize."

Melody's lips pinched even further and her scowl deepened.

CR ƧƆ

Ray was sure of one thing. Lily could make biscuits twenty-four hours a day and he'd be happy. It was like biting into a little bit of heaven with butter on it. He had to bite his tongue to keep the moan inside as it rose up his throat.

The beans were tasty too. She must have added a few things to make them a little less plain. The unfortunate result of his usual cooking was plain food. Too plain. This was the best meal he'd had in his kitchen in years.

Melody dug in with gusto, sopping up the beans with her biscuits and shooting dirty looks at Lily.

"Mel, do you have something you need to say to Miss Wickham?"

She turned her scowl on him and shook her head.

"Get it done, girl."

She sighed heavily then proceeded to open her mouth, stuffed full of dinner, and apologize to Lily. He had all he could do not to slap his forehead.

"I appreciate the apology, Melody. Please remember not to speak with food in your mouth." Lily's response reflected a level of class he'd never achieve.

God, she was such a lady. Too much a lady for a Wyoming horse ranch. He was about to discuss her return to New York when she started talking.

"I'd like to start Melody's lessons the day after tomorrow. I thought it would be a fun idea if she showed me around the ranch tomorrow, perhaps introduce me to everyone. Maybe even take a ride into town to get some supplies. What do you say, Melody?"

A trip to town was a treat for Melody. He hadn't taken her there in years, not since she was three years old and some old biddy in the general store had pulled her skirt aside when Melody walked past. Ignorant bitch. He had decided then and there to keep Melody away from town as much as possible.

Melody's eyes lit up like stars in the sky.

"Town?" She turned to look at her father. "Can I, Pa? Really?"

"I don't see why not." Lily plowed on, heedless of anything but the sound of her own voice. "We definitely need to purchase supplies, and I need a new pair of shoes. We can also look into some material to make new clothes. Do you want to learn how to sew, too?" She talked as if he wasn't even there.

"Sewing is women's work," Melody scoffed.

"Oh, but the things you can do if you know how to sew. Not just clothes, but dolls, toys, maybe a new neckerchief for your father. The possibilities are endless."

She spoke with such enthusiasm. Her whiskey-colored eyes shone with warmth and practically jumped with excitement. Lily had an aura of light around her. It was like looking at a force of nature. A force of nature who ran roughshod over him as he watched.

"Dolls are for girls."

"Yes, they are and I played with mine for hours on end. I even made them a little bed out of some scrap wood and sewed a blanket and clothes for them."

Ray could just see Lily as a young girl, putting her doll to bed, dreaming of being a mother some day. She said she was twenty-six. He wondered why she had never married. She obviously loved children.

Melody was interested in what Lily was saying, but he could tell she was trying to stay away from her. It wasn't going to be that easy.

"Dolls are for girls," Melody repeated, a little less strongly.

Lily shrugged. "Perhaps we can make something else then. I will need some help finishing my list of supplies though. Will you help me?"

Melody thought about it, then nodded. "You might ferget something or add stuff we don't need. Girlie stuff."

"You're absolutely right. I don't want to overrun the ranch with girlie stuff. Your father may end up with pink shirts or a purple feather on his bonnet. Imagine how the horses and cows will react to that."

Ray bit back a laugh, watching Melody do the same. Lily was going to be good for her. Then Lily turned her smile on him and his heart beat for the first time in over five years. A great big thump that echoed through his body like a rumble of thunder.

"Would you mind escorting us ladies to town tomorrow?"

Without realizing what he was doing, Ray nodded.

He should be scared. He should be terrified. He knew, without a doubt, Lily Wickham was going to change his life.

CR SO

"I still don't like her."

Ray swallowed the sigh that wanted to escape. He was trying to put Melody to bed but she resisted every move he made with ridiculous ease. Made him wonder how the hell his five-year-old daughter knew how to outwit him.

"You don't have to like her. You just have to listen to her. She's going to teach you all kinds of things, like how to read and cipher."

Melody sat on her bed in her small white nightdress, arms crossed, with a pout to her lips like any other little girl. Her dark eyes were full of sadness, anxiety and unknown deeper emotions. She wasn't like other little girls, yet she was. So damn young and vulnerable, yet possessing a strength inside no one her age had.

"I can read."

"The name on a bag of seed doesn't count. You can't read books yet. Miss Wickham will teach you."

He tried to tuck her in, but she sat back up immediately, dark locks flying.

"I don't want her to teach me. I want it to be just you and me, Pa, like it always was. She made me wash and she scrubbed me raw."

He didn't see it coming. Melody burst into tears, shocking the hell out of Ray. She was not a child who cried often, and here she was with great, gusting sobs, shaking like a fall leaf in a winter storm. He scooped her up and put her little body on his lap. He rubbed her back and crooned nonsense words into her ear until the shaking subsided, and her sobs reduced to little hiccups.

"It's okay, honey. Everybody gets scared and upset sometimes."

She snuffled loudly and wiped her nose with one hand. "Even you?" she said into his chest.

He smiled at her. "Even me."

She lifted her tear-stained face and looked at him suspiciously. "When?"

He rubbed his thumb on her cheek to erase the tears. "I remember once when Uncle Jack and Aunt Rebecca were lost in a blizzard. I was plenty scared even after we found them, because they were very sick from being outside in the cold so long."

She tilted her head and seemed to be contemplating his answer. "Okay. I believe you."

Melody tucked her head back under his chin. It was a good thing too, because he couldn't keep the smile back if he tried. She was way too smart for a five-year-old. Sometimes he wondered if she was fifty instead of five. She had an old soul, one who had seen much and carried those lessons deep down in her heart.

"If I ask you to, will you make her go home?"

"That's not a fair question, Mel."

Although he wanted to send Lily home the second he saw her, he found himself convincing his daughter to let Lily stay.

"She came a very long way to be your teacher. We can't send her back two thousand miles because you got mad that she made you wash. Give her a chance, okay?"

Melody was silent, curled up in his lap like a kitten. He was beginning to think she fell asleep when he heard a little sigh escape.

"One chance, no more."

He shook his head. "Let's take it one day at a time."

She sniffed and didn't respond.

"Now you need to go to bed, it's way past your bedtime, as usual."

He stood and laid her back down on the bed, tucking the blanket and quilt up around her chin. The chin that stuck up like a weapon when she was angry. The only part of Melody that reminded him of her mother, Regina. A fact he was heartily glad of.

He leaned down and inhaled her scent, a fresh scent, a smell that invoked so many memories. Restless nights, sloppy kisses, little hugs, and a million reasons why he would never have traded being a father for the world. A surge of love for his daughter nearly overwhelmed him.

"You're squeezing me too tight, Pa."

He released her and kissed her forehead. "Sorry, Little Note."

"I'm not a baby anymore. Don't call me by that baby name."

Ray chuckled and stuck his nose in her neck, sniffing like a puppy. Melody giggled and scrunched up her neck, trying to get away. He just dug further, sniffing harder and faster. She giggled louder and started pushing at his shoulders.

"Stop it, stop it!"

He pulled back and landed a big, noisy kiss on her cheek. "Even if you want to be called Mel, you're still my Little Note, my Melody."

Melody rolled her little eyes. "Okay, if you want to."

He gave her a quick hug and dropped a kiss on her forehead, then stood and gazed down at her. She looked so damn small lying in that bed.

"Good night, honey."

"Night, Pa. I love you."

Ray's throat pinched every time he heard his daughter say that. "I'll see you in the morning."

℘ ℘

Standing outside her room in the hallway, Lily hadn't meant to eavesdrop, but she heard part of their conversation anyway. It was obvious Ray loved his little girl a great deal. She wondered why Ray didn't tell Melody he loved her. A simple response, one Lily had never heard herself. Why Ray didn't tell his daughter was none of her business, of course.

She was walking down the hall toward the bathing room when he popped out of Melody's room like a dark shadow. She stifled a yelp and jumped a good foot off the floor.

"Holy sh-sheep!" she squeaked. "You scared a year off my life."

"Holy sheep?" he asked in a whisper with amusement in his voice.

The gloom of the hallway hid his eyes, but she saw his mouth. He had very sensual lips for a man.

"It's, um, better than other, less appropriate words," she whispered back.

That sounded stupid even to her own ears. She'd better control her outbursts and that included her choice of vocabulary words. He had absolutely no idea where Lily was from and she was determined to keep it that way.

He grunted and went to move past her.

"I hope you don't mind that I suggested a trip to town."

He stopped right next to her. They were practically shoulder to shoulder. She felt the body heat leap from him to her.

"I wish you had asked me first, but done is done."

He certainly didn't sound happy about it. She didn't know what to say to that. It had seemed like a good idea when she thought of it. Perhaps Ray didn't like to go into town. That was obvious by the state of his pantry.

"We can do it another day if you'd rather."

He rubbed his hand down his face. "No, tomorrow is fine. Doesn't matter what day you pick. It will be the same."

Ray moved away and Lily felt the loss of heat. She swayed toward his wide back—her body seemed to have taken over where her brain stopped working.

She watched him walk away, admiring the long-legged stride and firm steps. He walked like a man used to the world getting out of his way.

CHAPTER FOUR

Ray walked away from Lily like his ass was on fire. He had to move quickly or he was in danger of slamming Lily up against the wall and wrapping himself around her.

He had felt an almost violent urge when she'd come so close to him—a primal reaction to her nearness, something he'd never experienced before with a woman. Even Regina. With her, he'd been led around by his dick without a thought in his brain besides her.

With Lily, a jolt had shot through him, an impulse to lay his hands on her. There had been a moment when he was sure his willpower would fail him. He practically ran away like a yellow-bellied coward. Who knew what she thought of him now.

Ray marched into the cold night air and slipped his coat on. His breath puffed out in a cloud in front of him. He cursed himself for not bringing his hat and gloves, but there was no way in hell he was going back in the house yet. After he stepped off the front porch, his boots crunched on the hard-packed snow as he stalked into the night.

Ray needed some time to wilt the raging hard-on in his trousers. He walked toward the barn and corral, listening to the soft whinny of horses and the whistle of the wind in the bare trees. He looked up at the sky and saw a million points of light twinkling in the velvet blackness. The moon hung low in the sky, so close he swore he could reach out and touch it. It was a brilliant white, lighting up the front yard and bathing the night with a soft glow.

Why her?

Why Lily?

No question she was beautiful, but no more beautiful than other women he'd known. Lily was also smart, but godawful clumsy. After making two horrendous messes in the kitchen, which she'd cleaned up, she broke a candlestick in the living room. She also seemed to trip over her own feet a lot.

Aside from all that, Lily was there to teach his daughter and take care of his house. Not service his carnal needs.

Ray reached the barn and opened the side door, slipping inside as quietly as he could. He let his eyes adjust to the blackness of the barn, then made his way over to Shadow's stall.

The big stallion had belonged to his younger brother, Logan, who had been murdered nine years ago. Although heading toward twelve years old, Shadow was still the best damn horse Ray had ever owned. The gray equine was part Appaloosa, part something else.

Shadow whickered when he scented Ray. He moved closer to the horse, laying his head against his great neck and sighing.

What the hell was he going to do about Lily? Keep his distance, that's for sure. He hoped Melody took to her. It had taken him nearly a year to find a woman willing to come out to the Wyoming wilderness. At the time it seemed like a fluke that a governess from New York was coming. Unbelievable enough he kept expecting her acceptance of the position to be a joke, so he'd let her come.

Now he felt like he was worse off than before she arrived. If that were possible.

He stroked Shadow's neck until he felt his self-control reasserting itself. Being around horses always had a calming effect on him. With one last pat, he moved away from Shadow and walked down the rest of the barn, doing a quick check on the horses.

When he was satisfied all was well, he went to the door and stepped back outside. The moon had risen a bit higher in the sky, illuminating the rear of the house.

And Lily.

Shit.

She was leaning out her window. Probably gazing at the sky as he had been doing. She wore something white, probably her nightdress, which glowed in the light of the moon. Her unbound breasts pushed up against her arms as she leaned on the windowsill.

Sweet Jesus.

Something else hit him even harder. Her hair hung down around her like a dark, lustrous curtain—wavy, full, and as tempting as any sight he'd ever seen. His dick was suddenly awake again with a vengeance, straining against his pants and snarling.

As he watched, she leaned a bit further out the window, twisting her head to see more of the sky. Then she leaned out too far and fell out the window.

CR SO

Lily tumbled outside and landed on her nose, which immediately made a popping noise, and a warm gush of blood bathed her face. The snow was absolutely freezing and her scantily clad body started shivering from tip to toes. She pushed up on her elbows and ended up shoving her hands deeper into the snow.

Yes, indeed, her fine graceful self just had to make itself known. Hopefully she could climb back into her window without anyone seeing her.

If only she hadn't been so hot, she wouldn't have opened the window. After the incident with Ray in the hallway, her entire body had been flushed and she felt a bit feverish. Odd, really, that reaction to a man. She had never had it before and hadn't expected it.

While she tried to cool off in the frigid air, she noticed the moon was bright in the dark sky. Naturally, she opened the window a bit more and leaned out to get a better look.

Then her natural grace took over, and she fell out the window into the snow.

The sound of boots rapidly running through the snow toward her dashed her hopes that no one had seen her.

"Lily! My God, are you all right?"

She turned her head and peered at Ray in the darkness. Might as well be honest. "No, I think I may have broken my nose. And I can't seem to get out of this snow. I'm afraid frostbite will be a possibility if I don't figure how to get back on my feet."

Before she could blink, strong arms lifted her effortlessly and she found herself being carried by Ray. It was dark enough she couldn't see his expression under the shadow of his hat, but she had no doubt it was not a happy face.

"Thank you."

Lily tilted her head back and pinched the bridge of her nose to stop the bleeding. Her nose was really the least of her concerns. Ray Malloy was the biggest.

He opened the door and brought her inside, kicking the door closed behind him. She had the insane notion of a groom carrying his bride over the threshold and she started laughing. The more she tried to stop, the harder she laughed.

"I'm not sure what's so damn funny, but if you don't hush up, I'm gonna throw you back into the snow."

Ray set her on the sofa in the living room. He glanced at her white nightgown and immediately his eyes changed. The pupils dilated and a hazy glow surrounded the green. His nostrils flared and his lips tightened.

Lily thought it was blood that he saw, but when she looked at her nightgown, she realized the snow had turned the white garment transparent. He could clearly see her breasts and her nipples, which were puckered harder than a stone, as well as a hint of the dark hair between her legs.

Lily was never so embarrassed in her life. She didn't know whether to stop her nosebleed or cover herself, so she tried both. One arm landed over her breasts, while the other continued to pinch her nose.

"Do you think you could get me a towel, and perhaps some of that snow for my nose?"

His gaze snapped to hers and what she saw in his eyes made her breath stop. Raw, blatant desire. For her. A plump, on-the-shelf spinster with a shady childhood and a penchant for tripping over her own two feet. Lily felt an answering yearning in herself, a need to find out if what she saw, what she felt from him, was more than lust.

"I—"

"Let me get that towel," he said. Then he was gone before she could finish her sentence.

Lily started shivering. She didn't know if it was from the snow bath or the look in Ray's eyes when he stared at her nearly naked body.

She was afraid it was from the latter, and she had no idea what to do about it.

CR ℘

Ray stumbled into the kitchen and stared at the sink for a full minute before realizing he was standing there like a fence post holding up nothing but air. He grabbed a towel from the side of the sink and opened the back door to scoop up some snow.

Goddamn!

After getting himself calmed down enough to stop thinking about Lily, he had to see her just about naked. The raging erection in his jeans was about to bust a button or two. Maybe he should stuff the snow down his pants instead.

After wrapping the towel around the snow, he rubbed his cold hand on his face, and tried to regain at least a portion of his self-control. Life wasn't exactly orderly before Lily got here, but it wasn't this gut-wrenching, off-balance shit either.

Ray didn't like it because he apparently had no self-control when it came to Lily. He should have listened to his instincts at the train station and popped her beautiful ass on an eastbound train immediately.

Too late, too late, chimed in his demons. *She's in your blood.*

He grabbed a washrag from the sink and stalked back into the living room. Lily was pinching her nose with one bloody hand and trying to cover herself with the other. Made him feel like a horse's ass.

"Let's get you cleaned up." He sat on the edge of the sofa. "Hold the towel and let me wash the blood off."

She pulled her hand away from her nose and took the towel from him. Her whiskey-colored eyes watched him warily as he leaned closer. As gently as he could, he washed the blood away. Some of it had dried already so he had to rub a bit. She didn't make a sound, but she winced when he was too rough. He was a hell of a bad nurse.

When Ray touched the hand covering her chest, she squeaked a protest.

"Look, Lily, I'm not going to attack you. I just want to clean the blood off your hand."

She nodded and tentatively held out her hand. He didn't blame her for being wary since he barked and growled a lot. There wasn't much that was soft about him. He wiped the blood off her hand, trying not to notice her long, slender fingers. However, he couldn't help but notice she had calluses on her hands. The mark of a woman used to working, to making her own way.

His opinion of Lily Wickham went up a notch or two. Nothing Ray despised more than a princess who wanted to be waited on.

"Now switch hands and put the towel up on your nose. The snow should help with the swelling."

She did as he bade and he wiped her other hand off. When he finished, he gently pulled the towel away to look at her nose.

"I don't think it's broken."

He replaced the towel and sternly met her gaze.

"If you were Melody, I'd tan your hide for having the window open in the dead of winter. I could also say that you got exactly what you asked for, leaning out the window so far."

She scowled and looked put out. "I was hot... I mean, it was too warm in my room. The fireplace was putting out a lot of heat. It was only for a moment or two. I never meant... Well, truth is, I tend to be a bit clumsy."

She looked as if she thought he was going to spank her and put her in her room. The thought of her round ass beneath his hands had his imagination running straight into his trousers. An area that didn't need more attention.

"I noticed."

She sighed. "I'm afraid it's hard to hide. Do you...that is...you won't fire me because of my clumsiness, will you?"

Ray was taken aback. She thought he would fire her because she popped her nose in the snow? Or made a mess in the kitchen? Was she kidding?

"No. That's kind of a stupid question."

"It's most certainly not a stupid question. I can't tell you how glad I am to hear your answer. I've had some...difficulties with employers in the past with my graceless mistakes. I want you to know that I will replace anything I break."

"Nothing here is worth more than the wood it sits on, Lily. I wouldn't worry about it."

She smiled around the towel and her eyes sparkled with something like gratitude. She reached for his hands, and a thread of panic stung him.

"Thank you, Ray. I promise I will try to be more careful."

He stood abruptly. "I'll just go wash this out."

Leaving her with her mouth slightly open in surprise, Ray fled the room, the washrag clutched in his hand.

CHAPTER FIVE

The ride to town was not a joyous trip. Melody glared at Lily the entire time because Lily had made the girl wash up again and comb her hair. The only fortunate thing was Mel had no dresses to wear so that battle waited for another day.

Ray sat like an angry bear on the wagon seat. He didn't say anything, not even "Good Morning" when Lily greeted him. He simply nodded and looked off into the distance. As if he couldn't stand to look at her.

Lily tried to be cheerful, but it was difficult. She had a sinking feeling this trip was not going to turn out as fun as she'd hoped.

As they got closer to town, Melody began to get excited. She was sitting in the back of the wagon with her arms folded, then suddenly she was standing behind them. Her head between them, her black braids swinging back and forth, gently touching their shoulders.

"Are we almost there?"

Lily waited for Ray to answer. She thought they were close, but she had only made the trip once, in the opposite direction.

"Yes. Now sit back down," Ray grumbled.

Melody sat and within two minutes popped up again.

"Are we almost there?"

Lily had to bite her lip to keep from grinning at the long-suffering look on Ray's face.

"Yes. Sit down."

Melody disappeared from view and this time lasted five minutes before her little dark head was between them again. Her cheeks were pink from the cold and her eyes sparkled.

"I can see it. Look, Miss Wickham. Can you see it?"

For once, Melody actually spoke to Lily without cursing, grumping or complaining.

"Yes, I certainly do."

"There's so many buildings, Pa. I don't remember so many."

The wagon rolled into the outskirts of town within ten minutes, a bubbling five-year-old and her grimacing father on board.

"Hey, look, there's one of those draft horses. Gosh, that's so big. And there, a fancy carriage. It's black with red inside. That's so pretty."

She went on and on until Ray growled at her.

"Enough, Mel. Jesus please us, could you be quiet for five minutes?"

Melody's face reflected hurt as she sat back down and folded her arms again, her enthusiasm dampened by her father's impatience. Lily didn't say anything, but she gave Ray a glare of her own.

"Don't say a word," he warned.

"I wasn't planning on it. I think you know how I feel."

Ray pulled the wagon up to the general store and set the brake. After hopping down, he held his arms out for Melody. Sticking her nose in the air, she ignored him and jumped. Lily thought she saw a small grin play around his mouth when he shook his head and picked her up, snuffling her neck. Melody squealed, laughing at her father's antics.

"Stop, Pa, stop!"

He gave her a big smacking kiss on her cheek and set her down. Lily's heart went pitty-pat at the sight of that small grin on his face. She hadn't seen him smile or even come close to it, and this, well, this just told her how handsome he would be when he did smile. It would be enough to knock her to her knees.

"I have to go to the blacksmith, Mel. You stay with Miss Wickham at the store until I get back."

Melody rolled her eyes and stuck her hands in the pockets of her overalls.

"Yes, Pa."

"I'll need you to make sure I don't buy the wrong items on the list. You helped me write it after all," Lily said as she tried unsuccessfully to get down from the wagon while holding a basket. "Ray, could you…"

He glanced at her, and she swore he looked embarrassed at forgetting her. Within moments, he stood beneath her. He reached up and took her by the waist. His large, strong hands caused a ripple of familiar awareness in her body. An awareness of him as a man. And she as a woman.

Ray set her down matter-of-factly and removed his hands. She could still feel the echo of his touch and she shivered.

"Get what you need in the store."

With that gruff sentence, he strode down the snowy street away from them. Lily turned to Melody who eyed the door to the store like it was a threatening, scary place.

"Are you ready, Melody?"

She glanced up with her deep, dark eyes and nodded once.

CR SO

They entered the store with a swirl of chilly air chasing them. Lily pushed the door closed behind them and stamped her feet to get the circulation going. Melody stuck to her side like a cocklebur.

"Can you hold the list for me?"

Lily handed the paper to the girl who took it with a shaking hand. Lily bent down and met her eye to eye and saw uncertainty and fear.

"I've never been here before either, Melody. But I think if we stay together, we can get everything on the list before your father comes back. Will you help me?"

Melody nodded again.

"Okay, let's take a look at the list."

Lily brought an empty basket for smaller items. As they shopped for such things as thread and needles, she let Melody put them in the basket. Larger items were put on the counter until they had a big pile of supplies. She read each item aloud with sounds elongated. Soon the girl recognized the sounds and tried to read them herself.

The small triumph thrilled Lily. Melody demonstrated a keen intelligence and the ability to be an apt pupil.

"I want to get you a book to practice reading." Lily led the girl toward the books in the front of the store. Lily was pleased to find a McGuffey's Reader. "This is an excellent first book for a smart little girl like you to learn to read."

"I ain't little."

Other than sounding out letters, this was the first sentence she had spoken the entire time they'd been in the store.

"I'm sorry. You're absolutely right. You are a young lady now."

Melody scowled like her father, but took the book Lily held out to her. She could not hide the excitement in her eyes even if she tried. Lily smiled.

"Now let's go find some material to make new clothes and some curtains. That's our last item on the list."

"Girlie stuff."

Lily shrugged. "Maybe, but I would still like your help."

Melody rolled her eyes. "Fine."

With such ringing enthusiasm, they went over to the table holding the bolts of cloth. Lily noticed the book clutched tightly in Melody's hands. As they went through each pattern, she asked the girl her opinion on everything.

It took a lot longer than Lily intended, but she wanted to make sure Melody felt included.

"I think we've picked out all the cloth we need. Let's go ask the nice lady to cut it for us."

Lily approached the counter with trepidation. Not once in the fifteen minutes she'd been in the store had they been spoken to.

"Good morning," Lily said with a smile.

The woman behind the counter was middle-aged with blonde hair in a tight bun. Her blue eyes weren't unfriendly, but they weren't warm either.

"Good morning."

"Would you be kind enough to assist me with some cloth?"

The woman looked at her, then at Melody.

"You're not from around here. She yours?"

"She is my pupil. I am her governess."

The woman nodded and came around the corner. She was slightly taller than Lily with a body softened by age. She wore a light-blue striped dress and a white apron around her slender waist.

"Show me what you want cut."

Inwardly shrugging at the other woman's brusqueness, Lily followed her back to the table with the cloths.

As they were getting the last bolt cut, the door opened with a tinkle of the bell and a young voice rang out, "Hey, look, isn't that the Indian bastard?"

 C3 80

Ray headed back to the wagon with the new hinges for the barn door. He stared at the snow as he walked, trying to sort out his thoughts. Lily sure put a knot in his tail and he was having a hell of a time untying it. He dropped the hinges into the back of the wagon and trotted up the steps into the general store.

As he stepped in, he heard Lily's voice. It was angry, but controlled. His stomach tightened at the thought that someone was bothering Lily or Melody.

"I'll thank you to watch your language in public, young man. That was a rude and unkind comment to make."

"He's just telling the truth, lady," said a youth of about fifteen with a red face and too long hair. He stood next to a smaller boy with dark hair and flashing eyes.

"Regardless of whether or not it was the truth, his manners are deplorable and he owes this girl an apology."

Lily was magnificent. She looked like a lioness, all fierce and protective. Of his cub. Her whiskey eyes shot sparks at the two boys.

"I ain't apologizing."

She took Melody by the hand and straightened her shoulders. Her glorious breasts thrust out and her chin stuck up.

"Then you, sir, are no gentleman. I will go straight to the sheriff and file a complaint."

Panic swamped the boy's eyes. "Don't go to the sheriff, lady. My pa will whoop my ass so hard I won't be able to sit down for a week."

"Then I suggest you apologize and work on improving your language."

She might be small, but she packed a big wallop.

"Sorry," he mumbled, then fled the store with his friend in tow. The two of them cursed under their breath.

Lily hadn't noticed him. "Are you okay, Melody?" she asked.

Melody nodded. "They weren't very nice."

"No, they weren't, but they won't bother us again."

Damn straight they wouldn't. Even if they didn't want to mess with Lily again, Ray would kick their goddamn asses if they bothered his Melody or Lily one more time.

"Let's get all our purchases together and check them off the list, okay?"

Melody whispered, "Okay."

Ray noticed she still held Lily's hand with a book clutched in the other. Melody saw Ray standing by the door and the look in her eyes was like a punch in the gut. Whatever those boys had said was hurtful.

Goddamn it! That's why he avoided town. Small-minded morons, all of them.

"Hi, Pa."

"Hello, Ray." Lily tried to smile, but it was obviously forced. "I think we have everything if you want to assist us with tallying the bill and taking everything to the wagon."

Ray nodded and went toward them, resisting the urge to grab them both up in an embrace.

After they settled up with a glaring Mrs. Goodson, they loaded the wagon and headed home. He didn't dare tell Lily the storekeeper was his ex-mother-in-law, and that she hated him intensely. A feeling returned tenfold. Another reason he didn't like to go to town. Everything reminded him of his failed marriage and the betrayal of his wife—a wife who made a fool of him and destroyed his life.

CR ℘

The mood had grown somber again with Melody quiet as a mouse, and Lily very pensive. Ray didn't talk much anyway so it was no stretch for him to not speak.

As they rolled along the snowy road with the sunshine warming them, Lily suddenly turned and looked at Melody.

"Do you know any songs?"

"No."

He couldn't see Melody, but he could practically feel her shaking her head no. There wasn't much music in their house.

"Do you want me to teach you any?"

"No."

"Do you mind if I sing one?"

"I don't care."

Such enthusiasm. He really needed to get Melody to work on her manners.

All thought was knocked from his head when Lily started singing "Amazing Grace". The absolute perfection of her notes, of her voice, nearly made his heart weep. It had been so long, *so long*, since he had seen, heard or felt anything so beautiful. When she launched into the second chorus, he found himself humming along in tune with her. His bass blended perfectly with her soprano.

When the last note echoed into the winter sky, he felt a loss. He wanted her to sing again, but didn't know how to ask. Melody saved him.

"That one was okay. Do you know any more?"

She did. In fact, she knew a lot of songs. She sang all the way home, everything from hymns to ballads to "O Susanna". It was the most relaxing two hours Ray had spent in many years...at least six. He was surprised to see the ranch house come into view.

"Home already?" said Lily.

As soon as the wagon stopped in front of the house, Melody jumped out and took off. Ray grimaced and then sighed.

"Was it something I said?"

Ray shook his head. "She's probably still upset about what happened in town."

"Perhaps I should talk to her?"

"No. She just needs time to herself." He paused, then wrapped the reins on the brake handle and turned to look at her.

Lily was beautiful. Her silly blue hat some nun had knitted for her covered her hair, but it made her face that much more incredible. Long, lustrous lashes framed her whiskey-colored eyes. Her cheeks were pink from the cold and her lips, oh God those lips, were as red as berries. He was in trouble and sinking fast.

"What did they say?" he blurted.

"What did who say?"

"Those boys at the store. What did they say that was so rude?"

Lily lowered her gaze to her matching mittens and fiddled with them a bit. "I'd rather not say."

"I don't give a rat's ass if you'd rather not. Tell me what they said."

She looked at him and scowled, but remained silent.

"Don't push me, Lily. I can *make* you tell me."

He swore he saw a shudder slide through her body.

"You're a bully."

"Get used to it. Tell me. Now."

She threw her hands up in the air. "Okay, they called her an Indian bastard, then one of them pointed at me and called me a whore."

Ray's fists clenched so hard, he swore his knuckles went out of joint.

Those little fucking bastards.

He hadn't realized he said it out loud until she spoke.

"That may very well be, but I believe I handled them okay."

"Don't expect me to apologize for cursing."

"I won't."

He leaned back, cocked his head to one side and looked at her. She hadn't even flinched when he'd cursed.

"Aren't you a nun?"

She laughed, a tinkling sound that tickled over him like a feathery caress. "No, I just lived with nuns. They were my teachers."

He grunted. "So you're not a nun, but you lived with them. Yet cursing doesn't bother you."

"I've heard worse than that. I became somewhat…immune to it."

Now he was really intrigued. "I thought you grew up with nuns?"

"I didn't always live at the orphanage with the nuns. I arrived there when I was eleven."

He pictured Lily at eleven, awkward and scared, with her bright eyes trying to adjust to living with a bunch of nuns. Probably even clumsier at that age if it were possible.

"Where did you live before that?" It wasn't usually like him to be so curious, but he couldn't seem to stop himself. Ray wanted to know more.

"I'm getting cold now. Could we unload the wagon and go inside?"

Oh, so that was her game. Obviously she didn't want to answer the question.

"Don't think I'm going to forget about this conversation," he warned.

"I wouldn't dream of it."

He scowled then jumped from the wagon into the hard-packed snow. His boots squeaked as he walked around to the other side to help her down. The minute his hands touched her, another jolt of awareness hit him. It was as if his body smelled her, like a dog scenting his bitch.

He removed his hands as quickly as possible.

"I'm sorry they called you a whore."

She shrugged and walked past him. "I've been called worse than that."

She took her basket full of small goods and her new boots from the back of the wagon and went toward the house. Ray stared at her retreating back.

She'd heard worse cursing. She'd been called worse than a whore. She lived with nuns as a young woman. Where was she as a child? Who was calling her worse names than a whore? And why?

CR ЯO

Lily concentrated on putting the supplies away where they belonged. As Ray brought in each bundle, she had to focus on what she was doing or she might do something she'd regret.

Like blurt her life story to him. Something she *never* wanted to do. There was too much pain and humiliation in her past. She didn't want it to taint her present. It was bad enough he knew how clumsy she was. He didn't need another excuse to fire her.

The truth was she liked Wyoming. She liked the wide open spaces, the clean air, and the man. She didn't know why. He was gruff, rude and a bit of a bully. Her head knew that, but her heart seemed to be galloping off on its own way.

Lily suddenly realized it was getting dark and she hadn't even started dinner. She pushed the beans onto the shelf in the pantry and ran back into the kitchen.

Straight into Ray who was carrying in the last of the supplies. She slammed into him with all the grace of a running cow. He dropped the bag of coffee beans, trying to catch her, but her momentum kept her going until she fell over backward with Ray close behind. She landed on the floor with an awful thump to her head that made her see stars. Coffee beans scattered everywhere in a symphony of plings.

All the breath was driven from her lungs as his body pressed against her from head to toe. He was so *hard*. There wasn't an inch of softness on this man. She had only touched a man once in her life, long ago, but he had been flabby. Ray was as hard as a block of wood. A block of wood lit by tinder, scorching her with heat.

Ray tried to scramble off her, but he slipped on the coffee beans and fell back down. His head smacked painfully into hers.

"Jesus Christ!" he shouted.

"I'm sorry."

He planted his hands on either side of her shoulders and pushed up. His eyes were alight with unnamed emotions and a bit of frustration.

"Are you all right?"

She nodded, suddenly aware her breasts were inches from him, and her lower half pushed against his. His cock lengthened and hardened, then twitched. A lick of fire leapt through her.

Her eyes stung as she held his stare. His heart thumped in tandem with hers, each racing at an accelerated pace. His pupils dilated and he licked his lips.

Before she knew what was happening, he kissed her. She closed her eyes and felt the earth shift beneath her.

His lips were firm—like him—yet supple, moving back and forth, teasing, tickling. Lily started kissing him back and discovered kissing was a hot, wet, incredible experience. Her entire body came alive under his. Heat raced through her from not only the kiss, but the full body contact. Her nipples were hard and aching, pressing against his chest.

When his tongue touched her lips, licking lightly, knocking on the door to be let in, she started in surprise. Lily was about to open her mouth when a small voice shrieked, breaking the spell like a bucket of ice water.

"What are you doing to her, Pa?"

Lily broke the kiss and stared up at Ray. Regret, confusion and desire swirled in his eyes. She felt her cheeks turn scarlet as he hopped to his feet. Lily stood with a little less grace, fortunately without falling again.

"Goodness gracious, I've made a mess. Look what I did, Melody. I bumped into your Pa and started to fall. He tried to catch me and he ended up falling too."

She forced herself to laugh lightly when she felt anything but light of spirit. Ray stomped over to the pantry.

"Then he dropped the coffee and it made a mess. Goodness gracious."

She tried to ignore Ray as he retrieved a corn broom and swept up the coffee with jerky strokes.

"Help me get this up, Mel."

Melody stared at Lily suspiciously, but knelt down on the floor and started scooping the beans back into the burlap bag.

Lily escaped to the stove and, with trembling hands, stoked up the fire until it burned brightly. By the time a few minutes had passed, she felt more in control of herself.

She turned and found Ray with the bag of coffee beans, alone.

"I didn't intend on doing that," he said.

"I know. I didn't either." She clutched her hands together in front of her. For some reason, she had a strong urge to touch him.

"Do you want me to apologize?" His voice was tight and curt.

She shook her head. "No. I…I kissed you back."

He nodded, gripping the bag tightly. "That you did. It's been quite some time since I kissed a woman, Lily, but that…that was…incredible."

With that, he disappeared into the pantry, then out the back door before she could absorb what he'd said.

The kiss was incredible. *Incredible.*

Lily couldn't contain the smile that spread over her face. She'd never been incredible in her life. Her heart felt immeasurably lighter as she started making supper.

ଔ ଌ

"Pa, why were you kissing Lily?"

Ray was expecting it, but had hoped it wasn't going to happen. "Men and women kiss sometimes, Mel."

"I know, but they're married. You're not married, are you?"

He tucked the covers around her and kissed her on the forehead.

"No, we're not married."

"You're not going to get married, are you?"

"Melody, would you please drop the subject? We kissed, yes. It was just that. Only that. A kiss. We're not married and we don't plan on getting married. Ever."

Melody scowled at him and opened her mouth to speak.

"Don't even think about it," Ray warned.

She closed her mouth and rolled over to her side.

With one last kiss for his daughter, Ray turned out the lamp and left the room. As he stepped into the hallway, his gaze strayed to the bedroom next door.

Lily's room.

His imagination exploded with thoughts of her white nightgown and the soft, womanly curves it held. Now he was tortured by the fact he knew exactly what those curves felt like against him. What her lips felt like against his.

His dick pressed hard against his trousers, stretching and yowling. It was going to be a long, lonely night.

CHAPTER SIX

The next morning was cloudy and the cold sharp as a knife. It looked like snow, so Ray kept both of his hands at the ranch doing repairs. Clyde worked on the corral fence, and Rafe helped Ray replace the hinges on the barn door. Neither one of them liked to talk much, which suited Ray just fine. He wasn't much of a conversationalist.

Both Clyde and Rafe had originally worked for his father and came to work for him six years earlier when he set up his own ranch, the Double R. Of course, now it was the Single R, but the branding had already been done by the time Regina left. Now it was a reminder to him about how devious women could be.

"Hold the frigging door straight, Rafe."

"I am. How about you get your ass in gear and put the hinge on there, boss?" Rafe shot back.

Rafe was around Ray's age, with dark black hair and steel gray eyes. He had a jagged scar that ran the length of one cheek from his eyebrow to his jaw. He never smiled. Ray privately thought it was because of how the scar would twist a smile into something that might scare small children.

"Shut your yap and hold the door," Ray grumbled

After he fitted the hinge in properly and was about to put a screw in, the music began. All of them froze like deer caught in a hunter's sights as the first notes floated over them.

Lily had found the piano and apparently played as well as she sang. Her beautiful voice and the lilting melody of "Barbara Allen" echoed through the air. He felt mesmerized by the perfection of the notes.

"Damn, who is that?"

Rafe's question knocked Ray out of his stupor.

"Mel's governess, Miss Wickham."

"Mel's what?" Rafe laughed. "Did you say governess? What the hell is this, a high-class ranch?"

Ray scowled at Rafe. "Shut up, Rafe. Mel needs a teacher."

"And you need to get laid. Do both and get yourself a wife."

"Not again in this lifetime. So mind your own fucking business," Ray growled.

"She sure can sing like an angel. If you don't want her, can I have a crack at her?"

A surge of anger struck like a lightning bolt, and Ray had to restrain himself from punching the other man.

"Not if you value your life."

Rafe shrugged one big shoulder. "Can't hurt to ask."

Lily launched into "I'll Take You Home Again, Kathleen" and the work stopped again. Damn, the woman had been blessed with a perfect voice. Ray felt almost dizzy and realized he was holding his breath so he could listen.

He threw the hinges and the screws on the snow and stalked toward the house. Rafe cursed at him, but Ray ignored him and continued walking toward his quarry.

CR ළා

Melody had finally come into the room. She stood near the side of the piano, staring at Lily with her unreadable dark eyes. Lily smiled and gestured for Melody to sit on the bench. Melody sidled up a bit closer, but didn't sit.

"Pa said my mama used to play," said Melody.

Lily missed a note, but fortunately picked up the melody again.

"Anyone can learn to play. It's wonderful to be able to play music."

Melody shrugged, then sat on the corner of the bench.

"Would you like to learn a simple song? How about "Twinkle, Twinkle, Little Star"? Do you know that one?"

Melody nodded slightly.

"Okay, put your finger on this key right here and press it twice."

Melody's small finger sat on the key and plunked it twice.

"Very good. Okay, now this key twice."

Within a few minutes, Melody had the notes down and played the song by herself. Lily clapped her hands.

"You did it. You did it!"

Melody looked at her and a tiny grin teased the corner of her little mouth.

"Can you teach me another one?"

"Why don't we—"

"What the hell are you doing?" came Ray's shout from behind them.

Both Lily and Melody jumped on the hard wood bench.

"Did I say you could play that piano? Don't you have something else to teach my daughter, like how to read?"

Lily turned to look at Ray while Melody disappeared like a gust of wind.

His eyes blazed green, his cheeks red from the cold. The dark hat sat low on his forehead, a gray scarf was wrapped around his neck, and the usual warm coat covered his broad shoulders. His gloved hands clenched and unclenched. Lily's gaze locked on those hands, wondering if she'd been wrong about Ray. Perhaps he did use his fists to get what he wanted.

After the initial shock wore off, Lily's anger decided to make an appearance.

"Thank you very much, Mr. Malloy. For the first time, your daughter was actually speaking to me, instead of running from me." She stood and approached him, her own hands clenched into fists. "And you had to come in here and rant at us. She scooted off without a sound. Now I'm going to have to work at her all over again. So thank you very much!"

Ray's mouth opened then closed. His eyes burned into her with restrained heat. Lily was shocked at her own words. She let her temper fly and ignored her better judgment that yanked on her hair, trying to hold her back.

"There are a lot of things I can teach her. Music is one of them. If you don't want anyone to use the piano, why don't you sell it or chop it up for firewood."

Lily turned and stalked out the room before she said something she'd *really* regret. Ray's hand on her arm stopped her. His eyes snapped with sparks of fury.

"You have no call to speak to me like that. You work for me, remember?"

She tried to dislodge her arm, but it wouldn't budge. He was too strong. She took a deep breath to give him a piece of her mind and inhaled a lungful of Ray instead. His scent carried a hint of outdoors, man, and that indefinable thing that was uniquely him. Her stomach clenched as her body remembered and craved his touch.

"I could say the same to you. *You* have no call to speak to *me* like that."

His grip loosened and he looked away for a moment. When he looked back, Lily saw a glimpse of some very old pain way down deep inside. A woman had caused that pain. She was sure of it. Now Ray ascribed all that was bad in the world to women. Poor Melody. No wonder she wanted to dress and act like a boy.

"Maybe I was a little rough, but my point is the same. Melody does not need to learn music."

"Yes, she does. Everyone should."

"No."

"Yes." Lily stuck her chin up and stood her ground.

"Goddammit, Lily! This is my house and—"

"Am I interrupting something?" came an amused voice from behind them.

Lily turned and saw a tall, beautiful woman with long, reddish-brown hair, curls flying every which way, bright green eyes and a grin. She wore a bulky brown coat and hat, and trousers. A baby was perched on her hip, a little cherub with gorgeous blue eyes, probably six-months old. Beside her stood two children, about five-years old, with pink cheeks and matching green eyes. They both had dark, lustrous black hair.

"Nicky. What the hell are you doing here?" Ray shouted.

"Good to see you too, Ray. We're on our way to the Malloy ranch. It's the twins' fifth-birthday party. Remember? We thought we'd stop and let them play with Mel for the day."

"Oh, right. I forgot."

"I'm sorry we missed Mel's birthday, but we brought her a gift. Logan insisted on carrying it."

Lily saw the boy holding a package wrapped in brown paper and twine.

"Let go of my arm," Lily whispered to Ray.

He started and immediately released her arm. Since he obviously wasn't going to introduce her, she did it herself. Holding out her hand, she walked toward the tall woman with a smile.

"Hello, I'm Lillian Wickham, Melody's new governess. Please call me Lily."

The other woman used her free hand to shake Lily's briefly.

"Howdy, Lily. Nicky Calhoun. I'm Ray's sister. These little ones are Logan, Rebecca and baby Frances. We call her Frankie, much to her father's displeasure."

Lily squatted down to greet the twins. "Hello there, Logan and Rebecca. I think Melody might be in her room. Would you like to go find her?"

Two dark heads nodded.

"It was very nice to meet you," she called as they scampered out of the room, leaving puddles of snow from their boots on the floor. Lily smiled and shook her head.

"They're beautiful children."

"Thank you. Ray, since you're standing there like a tree stump, why don't you go outside and help Tyler unhitch the team?"

Ray stomped out of the house without a word and slammed the door behind him.

"My brother doesn't get good marks for manners. I'm sorry he was so rude."

Lily waved her hand. "I've only been here a few days, but I already picked up on that. His bark is worse than his bite."

Nicky laughed. She had a deep voice, and her laugh was husky as well.

"You learn quickly. Are you the governess from New York that Mama was talking about? The nun?" Nicky set the baby on the rug in front of the sofa and took off her coat and hat. The baby had the same curly reddish brown hair as her mother. Nicky pulled out a few wooden toys from her coat pocket and gave them to little Frankie.

"Yes, and no. I am the governess from New York, but I'm not a nun. I lived at an orphanage run by nuns. Mother Superior was the one who recommended me for the position. She and your mother are old friends."

Nicky nodded as she took off her coat and boots, setting them by the fireplace. "I remember her letters arriving and Mama going off on her own to read them. They were childhood friends, I think."

She plopped down on the rug next to her baby. Lily decided she liked this sister of Ray's very much.

"Why don't I make some tea?" Lily offered

"Sounds wonderful. I'm about chilled through."

Lily went into the kitchen and put water on to boil. While she got the teacups and tea ball ready, she talked to Nicky about her children. They were smart little scamps, apparently, who kept their parents on their toes. When the water was hot, she poured it into the teapot and brought a tray in with the tea and some biscuits from breakfast.

"Oooh, biscuits," Nicky exclaimed, snatching one from the tray. She broke off a piece and fed it to Frankie who gummed it, happily.

Lily set the tray on the table behind the couch, and poured two cups. She handed one to Nicky, then took one with a biscuit and sat on the sofa.

"So what was the argument about? You sure had him riled." Nicky chuckled.

Lily felt a blush creep around her cheeks that she tried to hide behind the teacup. "I'm sorry you heard that. I am not normally so sharp-tongued, but something about Ray just gets my dander up. He refused to allow me to teach Melody music and the piano. He was not particularly polite about it either."

Nicky's smile disappeared. "The piano. That figures. It belonged to Ray's ex-wife, Regina. I don't know why he didn't get rid of it. Maybe he likes it as a reminder about the faithlessness of women."

"Ex-wife? I don't believe I've ever met anyone who was divorced."

Lily was completely intrigued. She knew she shouldn't gossip, but had the feeling whatever Nicky was going to say would be vitally important to her relationship with Ray Malloy.

Nicky sighed and ruffled her daughter's hair.

"I like you, Lily. I trust my instincts completely and they tell me that you're someone I can trust."

"Thank you. I feel I am trustworthy and any insight into why Ray is so…so bullish would be appreciated."

"Bullish. Yeah, that's a good word. He's got the temperament and the stubbornness of a bull, doesn't he? He wasn't always that way. I was gone when it happened, but somehow Regina got pregnant and forced Ray into marriage. I'm sure Ray thought it was the right thing to do."

Lily understood completely. Many couples anticipated the wedding night, but generally they were already engaged when they did.

"All through her pregnancy, Regina was miserable, whining and petulant. I never liked her, but after Melody was born and she abandoned both of them, I decided I hated her."

Lily sucked in a breath. "She abandoned them? Melody was just a baby then?"

Nicky nodded, grimacing. "She was two weeks old. I was pregnant with the twins and was trying to help, but she didn't want any of it. Told me to go to hell."

"Sounds like someone I could grow to hate as well."

"That's the truth. The thing is, and don't repeat this to a soul, we could all tell that Melody was not Ray's daughter."

"What do you mean?"

Not his daughter? How could that be?

"You notice that Melody has black eyes and black hair, right? Ray has brown hair and green eyes. Regina has blonde hair and blue eyes. Brown and blonde don't make black hair. And green and blue don't make black eyes."

Isn't that the Indian bastard? The boys' cruel words from the store echoed in her head. Ray's angry reaction. It all fit now. Poor Melody and poor Ray.

"Ray loved that little baby from her first breath, so don't think she isn't his daughter in his heart. He would move heaven and earth for that child."

Lily felt pain for Ray down deep in her heart. She understood all about abandoned children and mothers who don't care about their children. A surge of respect, admiration and just plain like for Ray burst through her. Now she felt like she could at least start to understand him.

If only she understood her reaction to him. And why she couldn't stop thinking about the kiss.

The door banged open and a huge man walked in with Ray close behind. He had the coolest blue eyes she'd ever seen, a perfect match to the baby's. This must be Nicky's husband. He was enormous. He took off his boots, coat and hat, shaking dark hair that reminded her of the twins. He was a very handsome man with a strong jaw and firm mouth.

He walked over, picked up baby Frankie, gave her a smacking kiss on the cheek, then proceeded to tickle her. Her baby laughter rang through the house, bringing smiles to everyone's faces. Never had Lily seen a father treat a baby with such affection. He sat in the chair and snuggled the baby under his chin.

"Who are you?" he said to Lily.

"Jesus please us, Tyler," Nicky admonished. "This is Melody's governess, Lily. Lily, this is my oafish husband, Tyler. Be nice, bounty hunter."

Tyler flashed a grin at his wife. "Always, magpie."

"Where's Noah?" Ray asked as he took off his coat.

"He's back at The Bounty Ranch. It's the first time he's been in charge while we're gone and he's about to bust his buttons over it." Nicky's eyes shone with pride. She turned to Lily. "Noah is our adopted son. He's just twenty and has become a man all of a sudden."

"It sure as hell wasn't sudden," Tyler said dryly.

Nicky stuck out her tongue and Tyler winked at her. Lily's gaze strayed to Ray who stood by the door watching the family with such naked longing on his face she had to look away. She felt the same longing, the same need to belong to someone. Seeing it up close was enough to make her heart prick with tears.

She tucked away her envy and spent the afternoon getting to know the Calhouns.

ଔ ଙ

Lily outdid herself on the afternoon meal. Ray ate so much stew and dumplings, he thought he was going to burst. Lord, that woman could cook.

The conversation floating around the table was punctuated with laughter and good-natured teasing. Lily fit right in with his family, and it seemed she and Nicky were as tight as ticks on a dog's ass.

He most certainly did *not* feel jealous of his sister.

When Lily brought out the dessert, a delicious chocolate cake, he found he was not quite as full as he thought. He hadn't had cake in so long.

"I understand that one somebody," she turned and winked at Melody, "and two other somebodies," she turned and winked at Logan and Rebecca, "are turning or just turned twenty."

The children all laughed and talked over each other to tell her they weren't twenty. They were only five. She pretended to look aghast and smacked her forehead with her hand as if she had just realized the error of her thinking. Ray was hard-pressed not to smile at her antics.

"Well, then, I made this cake for twenty-year-olds. Do you think it's okay to serve it to five-year-olds?"

They all chimed in with loud "Yes!" "Yeah!" and "Yup!" She looked doubtful, but went to cut the cake, then stopped the knife hovering over the chocolate confection.

"Are you absolutely sure?"

The children groaned and pounded their fists on the table. Tyler grinned, and Nicky laughed. Little Frankie sat on her lap, waving a spoon like a weapon and smiling happily at everyone.

Lily pulled out three candles from her pocket and stuck them in the cake. She struck a match and lit the candles one by one.

"For Melody. For Rebecca. For Logan. Is everyone ready? Okay, make a wish and blow out your candles."

The three children, all dark headed, leaned forward and blew with all their might on the candles. The candles fluttered, two went out, but Melody's was in danger of not going out. Without revealing herself to the girl, Lily leaned down and blew quickly, helping Melody's candle wink out.

Everyone clapped and yelled "Happy Birthday" to the joyous children who beamed like angels.

A sudden thought struck and Ray realized what he felt was happiness. There was no strife, no trouble, no fear dragging him down. At that very moment, he felt happy. Because of Lily. She brought silliness, laughter and her own brand of sass into his house.

What he felt for Regina passed long before they stood in front of a preacher. What he was beginning to feel for Lily was much, much deeper. It involved his heart, his mind and his soul.

Oh, shit.

He was definitely in trouble.

CR RO

The Calhouns left shortly after supper, and the house echoed with silence. After her nightly battle of the bath with Melody, Lily felt restless and antsy. She tried to concentrate on some mending, but her stitches were all crooked and she pulled them out three times before deciding enough was enough.

It was too cold to walk outside, and pacing in the living room just wasn't releasing her energy, but it was better than nothing. She had a feeling she knew the cause of her problem.

Family. To be part of and to witness everything that was the Calhoun family, ignited a yearning inside her that burned brightly. It's what she had been missing all her life. She knew it would fill the empty holes in her soul, in her heart. She loved the nuns to distraction, but they were never enough.

She wanted a husband. She wanted children of her own.

The front door burst open, startling her so badly she jumped a foot and yelped like a completely ninny. She tripped over the chair and ended up on her knees, painfully smacking them on the hard wood floor.

"Should I help you up, or pretend it didn't happen?" asked Ray as he closed the door.

Lily groaned at the pain shooting up from her knees. "This time, I think I'd like help up."

In a moment, Ray was beside her, gently lifting her to her feet. He held her steady when she wobbled a bit. His big hands felt wonderful on her waist, making her feel smaller than she really was. She knew she was plump, but he was so big, it didn't matter.

"Better?" he murmured near the top of her head.

She nodded. Lily realized he was mere inches from her. The heat from his large body quickly warmed her to dangerous levels.

"You smell like lavender."

"I use it in my bath." She looked up and met his gaze. To her surprise, she saw gentleness in his eyes, laced with a heady lust that jumped from him to her. Her breasts tightened and the nipples pebbled until they were almost painful. A pulse thrummed through her, carrying an age-old melody that sang between her legs, in her most secret place.

"What's happening, Ray?"

"Damned if I know, but I'm tired of fighting it."

His arms went around her and she was pulled up against his hard body.

Finally.

She reached up and wrapped her arms around his neck. In seconds, his lips found hers. They were at once hard yet soft, demanding yet gentle. She learned quickly how to nibble, lick and suckle. At the first touch of her tongue to his lips, he groaned from deep in his throat and held her tighter.

Lily felt her body opening like a flower in the morning sun. Her petals open to the life-giving warmth that was Ray.

His mouth covered hers and his tongue danced within her mouth. Caressing, exploring and teasing hers. When she moaned, he broke the kiss and held her to him. Her heart beat so hard, she was afraid even the horses in the corral heard it. His thundered against her chest like a train engine.

"I'll be damned if I can explain this, Lily. It's like I can't keep my hands off you." His voice was rough against her temple.

"Why did you stop then?"

His chuckle sounded more like a groan. "I don't believe in taking virgins on my living-room floor."

Lily opened her petals even further, stepping into the dangerous precipice that was her past. "What if I told you I'm not a virgin?"

Ray's entire body tightened at once, squeezing her so hard she could hardly catch a breath. He let go quickly.

"Is it true?"

"What if it were? Would you have stopped?"

He pulled back and held her at arm's length. His eyes were dark with passion and frustration, his mouth nearly white from strain.

"Is it true?"

"You answer my question first."

He released her completely and stepped away to run his fingers through his hair. Blowing out a huge breath, he put his hands on his hips and faced her. She could see the hardness of his erection in his pants. The thought that kissing her did that was nearly enough to make her grab him and kiss him again.

"You don't play fair."

She cocked her head and shrugged. "I don't know the rules of the game, so how can I know if I'm playing fair?"

"We need to do something besides discuss this."

Lily smiled. "We could go back to—"

"Besides kissing. Something *else*."

Lily frowned. "You change the rules all the time."

He kicked off his boots and they landed near the door. "My house. My rules."

Lily wanted to explore the feelings more deeply, but obviously Ray was done talking. He very clearly wanted to continue, but honor held him back. He thought her a virgin and respected her for that.

If only he knew the things she'd done as a young girl to survive, to try and please a mother who would never be appeased. If she admitted to not being a virgin, he would want to know why. She wasn't prepared to tell him.

"Can we play poker?"

She'd shocked him. He looked like she'd asked him to wear a pink dress and whistle *Dixie.*

"Poker?"

"It's a card game. Do you know how to play?"

He scoffed manfully. "Of course I know how to play. Do you?"

"Yes, I do."

He scowled. "Nicky knows how to play, but there is a very good reason why. I'm wondering how you know how to play."

Lily shrugged, butterflies dancing in her stomach, hoping he wouldn't ask too many questions.

"There are a lot of things an orphan learns to survive," she said that half-truth with a straight face.

Just accept me, Ray. Please.

"I've got a deck of cards in my room. Meet me in the kitchen in two minutes. I expect a late-night snack too."

He walked from the room with one last scowl at her. She let out a shaky breath and closed her eyes. Things were getting very complicated, very quickly with Ray Malloy.

When she'd left New York, she had no idea her life would be completely different within a week. Or that she'd find herself falling in love with a man whose heart was damaged almost as much as hers.

CR ‫ാ‬

Lily didn't really like horses. Okay, she was scared to death of them. Avoided them at all costs. However, she knew Melody loved them. On the second day of Melody's refusal to learn, Lily worked up enough courage to go out to the barn. The barn where the horses resided. The big, scary horses. Perhaps if Lily learned to be unafraid of horses, she could convince Melody to teach *her* about them, bridge an enormous gap that seemed unbridgeable.

Bundled in as many layers as she could get on without falling on her head, Lily strode out the door toward the barn. The wind whistled past her nose, instantly chilling her. She wished she had known just how cold Wyoming was. She'd have purchased more flannel.

Her boots squeaked on the snow as she walked. The Wyoming landscape in winter was very barren and bleak. The only bright spot she saw was the red barn. Not too bright though, it did house the enormous beasties called horses.

When she reached the building, she tugged on the door and stepped inside the gloom. The whiteness of the snow contrasted sharply with the darkness of the barn and it took several agonizing minutes before Lily could see properly. She imagined all sorts of horrible things happening to her while she stood there like a ninny, blinded.

After her eyes adjusted, Lily cautiously surveyed the large interior. It was relatively clean, although it definitely smelled of its equine residents. She stepped carefully, watching for piles of manure and any other nasty gifts one might find on a barn floor.

Several of the stalls were empty before Lily came upon a horse. It was a small black horse with a diamond-shaped white spot on its snout. It looked at her with dark, inquisitive eyes, but made no move to get closer to her.

"Well, hello there, Mr. or Miss Horsie. I, uh, am looking for Melody."

As soon as she heard her voice echo back to her, Lily's cheeks heated with embarrassment. Why was she talking to a horse? She took off her mittens with shaking hands and forced herself to step closer to the stall door. Her heart hammered in trepidation.

"You're not so big, are you? Are you a boy or girl?"

"It's a girl." Ray's voice behind her made Lily jump a foot in the air and screech like a little girl.

"Sweet Saints! Are you trying to scare me to death?" Lily gasped and pressed her hand to her palpitating heart.

Ray stood with one dark eyebrow cocked and a giant three-pronged fork in his hand. "Why the hell are you talking to the horse?"

Lily's bright idea now seemed like a stupid mistake. "I, um, that is…I just wanted to meet them."

Ray snorted. "Meet the horses? Did you expect them to curtsey or bow?"

His comments stung. "No need to be mean, Ray. I just meant that I hadn't seen any of the horses and since Melody liked them so much I thought…"

Ray nodded. "You thought you could talk to her about the horses."

"Something like that. You see…I'm embarrassed to admit this." Lily glanced at the small black horse who continued to stare at her. "I am afraid of horses."

She swore she heard Ray chuckle under his breath, but he covered it with a cough. Lily narrowed her eyes. "Did you just laugh at me?"

"No. I'm not one to laugh, that's a fact." He stepped closer to her and Lily's body immediately began to hum. Apparently just being near him fanned the flames of her sleeping desire. Since Ray was the one who would not consummate their relationship, Lily refused to move even an inch.

"Why are you afraid of horses?" he asked as he set the implement against the beam. In the gloom of the barn, his eyes were like dark forests of the unknown.

"When I was little, my family rode mules, never could afford horses. Once when I was about five, in Kansas, a horse kicked one of our mules to death in front of me. Vicious spiteful beast." She shuddered at the memory of the blood and the donkey's screams. "It was a sweet donkey named Annabelle that apparently took umbrage at a horse forcing himself on her. It was…frightening."

Ray stepped even closer. He took off his glove and cupped her chin. "No wonder you're afraid. Not too many are that mean, leastwise not in this barn. I keep all the greenbroke and wild ones out in the corral. Keep clear of those."

His thumb swept back and forth across her cheek. Lily forced herself not to lean into his hand, not to melt into a puddle at his feet. Her nipples already pressed into the layers of cloth, aching peaks of arousal.

"The horses in the barn won't hurt you." He was mere inches from her, his breath skittered across her lips. "Everything in here is friendly."

Before Lily could protest, his lips were on hers. The kiss was gentle, light, nearly a caress. Lily moaned and leaned toward him, hungry for more, desperate for him to stop. He reached a hand around her neck and pulled her closer. The passion from his body seeped through to her own, heating her so quickly, she perspired under the layers.

Lily grabbed his coat and pressed against him fully, chest to chest. Yet it wasn't enough. She needed more. Her hands landed on the buttons of her wool coat and suddenly he stepped away from her. Lily swayed from the loss of his heat.

"Holy shit. I told myself that wouldn't happen again." His voice rasped in the quiet barn.

"That's your choice, Ray."

"Dammit, Lily, we can't be kissing all the time or anything else. There isn't any future in it." He took off his hat and slapped his leg with it, his frustration as evident as the arousal in his trousers.

"I didn't say I wanted a future. I just wanted to see where it would lead," Lily lied. Oh, she definitely wanted that future, with enough force to crack her heart.

He narrowed his eyes. "I have trouble believing that. No woman just wants a tumble in the hay and nothing else unless she's a whore. You are no whore."

Lily pushed a stray hair off her face. "Thank you, I think."

"That didn't come out right. Oh, hell, why do I even try?" With that, he snatched the three-pronged fork and marched away, still cursing.

Lily's temper flared and she marched after him. He was in the last stall, picking up soiled hay and depositing it in a wheelbarrow. She tapped him on the shoulder. When he looked up in surprise, she took the fork, set it aside, then pushed him into the stall wall with a bang and kissed him.

It wasn't the hesitant kiss of two minutes previous. This was a possession. Dancing, sliding tongues, harsh breathing, pounding hearts. Lily put all her pent-up passion into a kiss that left them both gasping for air. When she finally let him loose, his eyes were wide. He licked his lips and Lily shuddered at the memory of his hot tongue in her mouth.

"Let's see if you can sleep tonight after that. My door will be unlocked."

Head held high, Lily forgot her reason for coming to the barn and walked proudly back to the house.

• • •

Ray watched Lily leave, digging his hands into the wood behind him to prevent him from following. If he had, they would end up in her bed with him buried inside her in two minutes flat.

Holy shit.

The last thing he expected was the mousy governess to turn into an aggressive woman. A woman who just kissed him so thoroughly, he could remember her teeth in order. His body pulsed with arousal and his dick pressed hard against his trousers, howling to be let loose. Being celibate for five years definitely had its drawbacks.

This was assuredly one of them. He simply couldn't bed Lily. It wouldn't be right and his mother would probably kick his ass if he did it.

Of course, the alternative was likely never sleeping again, or wearing out his hand trying to get to sleep.

"What the hell are you doing?" Rafe's voice rang out.

Ray shook his head like a dog. "Jesus Christ, she's going to be the death of me."

Rafe grinned and grabbed the pitchfork. "Ain't it a bitch?"

"Shut up, Rafe."

Ray had no idea how long he stood there, staring at the closed door after she'd left, but it was long enough to make Rafe howl with laughter. Damn, why couldn't the governess be old and warty?

Why did he get saddled with such a delicious, voluptuous, tempting siren? A siren who called to him so loudly, his ears rang with want, with need, and with regret.

CHAPTER SEVEN

Two weeks passed with Ray and Lily carefully trying to avoid being alone. Melody continued to evade Lily during the day. No matter how hard she searched, she could not find that little girl's hiding place.

She felt like a failure and dared not ask Ray for help. Each day she woke with the determination to find Melody and corner her into learning. Well, perhaps not corner her, but at least get her to start reading McGuffey.

It was Friday, nearly three weeks since she'd arrived in Wyoming. Lily sipped a cup of tea, staring out the kitchen window at the snow sparkling in the bright sunlight. In two days, they were headed to Ray's parents' house for the twins' birthday party. Melody talked little, but she did express, exuberantly, that she wanted to go to the party. Lily saw Ray wanted to say no, but he promised his daughter they would go. Lily was nervous about the trip.

What was the rest of Ray's family like? Would they like her? She obviously was not the governess Ray hired, or she would have gotten her pupil to sit down and learn once in a while. Instead of never. She was really working as a cook and housekeeper.

Being around Ray was more than a curious want. It had become a need. She needed to see him, hear his voice, brush up against him as he ate his breakfast. Each moment seemed stolen, somehow more valuable. She was on very shaky ground and hoped fervently the ground did not open up beneath her.

A knock at the door startled her and the hot tea splashed on her hand. After yelping from the pain, she set the teacup on the table and pressed her throbbing hand against the apron she had tied around her waist. The dress was one she had just made from beautiful green wool and she didn't want to ruin it.

The knock at the door sounded again, this time a bit more impatiently.

"I'm coming," she called out, then tripped over Melody's wooden puzzle. She nearly fell on her head, but kept her balance by grabbing the sofa.

The third knock was more of a bang.

"I'll be right there. Hold your water."

Good Lord! She sounded like a fishwife. Stifling a giggle, she walked to the door with as much dignity as she could summon. When she flung it open, she found two tall, big men who resembled Ray quite a bit. These must be two of the brothers she had heard about.

"Well, howdy there, ma'am. I'm Trevor Malloy and this here's my brother, Brett," one of them said as he took off his hat. "You must be Miss Lily."

Brett took off his hat and nodded. "Ma'am."

"Hello, Brett, Trevor. Please come in." She opened the door wider and they stepped in. Everyone in the Malloy family must be tall because these two were as big as Ray. Even Nicky was tall. Lily felt like a child next to this family.

"What brings you to the Double R?" she asked politely.

Trevor flashed a dazzling grin. Lily knew in a minute he was the charming brother. The one who could wiggle his way out of any situation by just opening his jar of honey. Brett was obviously the quiet one who was used to being in the shadow of his brothers.

"Our mama sent us over to escort you to the Malloy ranch. All of you. Everyone else is already there, including Nicky and Tyler and the kids. Mama expected you a few days ago."

It was news to Lily. She thought they were going over for the day, not to stay for several.

"That's very kind of you. Why don't you make yourselves comfortable while I go make some coffee?"

They both nodded their thanks and with one last melting grin from Trevor, she scooted into the kitchen. While she brewed the coffee, she decided she would find out when they needed to leave. With or without the stubborn Raymond Malloy.

CR SO

When he returned from checking the cows in the winter pasture, Ray saw two horses in front of the house. He cursed heartily after recognizing Trevor's and Brett's mounts. His meddling mother must have sent them.

As he stalked toward the house, he figured they must be inside. With Lily. Alone. For God knows how long. He picked up his pace. He was *not* running.

He threw open the door with a bit more force than he'd intended, crashing the door into the wall behind it. He heard a crunch and realized he'd have to patch the hole he just put in the wood.

"Hey, Ray, what're you doing? Trying to tear the door off?" Trevor smiled from his position on the couch. A cozy, comfy position with a mug of coffee and a cookie.

"Hello Ray," said Brett as he nodded. Ray noticed Brett did not hold a cup or a cookie, but sat stiffly on the couch beside Trevor. Ray slammed the door closed and whipped off his hat and coat.

Lily sat in the chair in a gorgeous green dress, whiskey-eyes glaring at him, teeth clenched.

"Your brothers tell me that you were expected days ago at your parents' house for the twins' birthday party," she added a bit too sweetly.

Shit. He'd forgotten about the party. His mother threw a shindig for all the grandkids when they had a birthday. It was the only party Melody got, and the only children who came were her cousins. Luckily there were a bunch of them now.

"Had some things I had to take care of here, boys." He saw Trevor's jaw tighten at the insult. At the age of thirty-one, he was no boy. Neither was Brett at thirty-two. Honestly, although Ray was thirty-six, he felt absolutely ancient compared to them.

He kicked off his boots and walked over on stocking feet to glare at his younger brothers.

"Don't you two have work to do around the Circle M ranch? What the hell you doing hanging around here and bothering Mel's governess?"

"She invited us in, Ray," Trevor responded smoothly with a crooked smile for Lily. "She warmed us up with coffee and cookies too."

Ray turned his glare to Lily. She raised her eyebrow at Trevor's antics, but didn't say a word.

"Where's Mel?"

"I haven't found today's hiding place yet."

Ray inwardly winced. Dang girl had more hidey-holes than a gopher. It was his damn fault. If he hadn't spooked her two weeks ago, she might be actually learning something from her teacher instead of hiding.

"She's as good as Nicky was, huh?" Trevor chuckled. "She could hide for near days before we found her. Little sh—scamp."

Lily stood with her usual grace and almost tripped over her skirt. Ray put a hand out to steady her, but Trevor had already grabbed her elbow.

"Easy there, little filly."

Ray's gut clenched at the way Lily returned Trevor's smile. Dammit all to hell! He was *not* jealous. He could've been in Lily's bed already if his conscience hadn't prevented it.

"Thank you, Trevor. Let me go check on that roast." She turned to look at Ray. "I'm making a pot roast for dinner with carrots and potatoes."

Ray's stomach rumbled in anticipation of Lily's cooking wonders.

"Can you ring the bell to see if Melody will come to eat?"

He nodded and walked back to the door. Stepping outside, he grabbed the triangle from beside the door and rang it three times.

As the last tinny sounds echoed across the snowy plains, he realized he was standing on the front porch, in the snow, in his socks.

Shit.

CR SO

After dinner, Ray bullied his brothers into going out to the bunkhouse with Clyde and Rafe to play poker. When Lily tried to interrupt him to say she'd like to play poker, he talked louder so no one heard her.

Brett and Trevor tipped their hats, said goodnight and thank you, then left to go join the poker game. Leaving her alone with Ray. The most stubborn, grumpiest man on the planet.

He sat at the table sipping a cup of coffee and going over the ledgers for the ranch.

She stood with her hands fisted on her hips until he looked up at her. "You were very rude to your brothers."

"You have a sassy mouth for a governess."

She shook her head. "I am always polite."

Ray snorted and returned his gaze to the ledger book. "And I'm always a ray of sunshine."

She couldn't help it. She laughed. It was pretty funny and awfully witty.

"I strive to always be polite."

"That I won't argue with."

"You were very rude to them. They could have stayed here for the evening."

He snorted a laugh and took a gulp of coffee. "You wanted Trevor to ogle you some more?"

Lily was nearly speechless with shock. "Ogle? *Me?* I think you may need spectacles, Mr. Malloy. I am nothing special, and certainly not worth an ogle."

When he glanced up again, his eyes blazed green fire. He set the mug down with a thump, then stood. He walked toward her like a predator stalking his prey, with a feral intensity that was almost physical.

"What you are, Miss Lillian Wickham, is a goddess wrapped up in wool. From your incredible lips to breasts that would more than fill my hands, all the way to your curves that keep me up at night. Literally."

By the time he reached her, she was trembling like a babe. The world seemed to have turned upside down. This man had her pulse pounding, her body moist in places she dared not mention, and her heart aching.

He cupped her cheek and his thumb stroked back and forth. Shivers traced the movement.

"I don't know whether to put you back on a train, put you over my knee and spank you, or throw you on my bed and make love until either one of us can't move."

Lily shuddered under the sensual assault. She had never experienced such raw desire before, the kind that grabbed hold and squeezed until you could hardly breathe. She leaned toward him as he lowered his lips toward hers. Her eyelids fluttered shut and she prepared for the assault.

It was like the fireworks she'd seen over the Hudson River. Flashes of light exploded behind her eyes as she was swept into his arms, and the kiss deepened. She mewled like a kitten when his big hands caressed and kneaded her behind.

His lips slipped off hers and slid down her jawbone, planting light kisses as he headed toward her ear. His rough tongue laved at her lobe. With each stroke, she felt an answering pulse between her legs. She pressed her body to his, rubbing her aching nipples against his hard chest. Tingles ran up and down her skin.

Lily was drowning in sensation. When he started sucking her neck, she realized she wasn't breathing. She pulled in a hard breath and let it out shakily.

"Ray..."

"Mmmm..." he murmured against her neck. When his hand landed on her breast, she moaned.

"Ray, we can't...do this...here," she managed to squeak out between gasps as the sensations continued to barrage her.

He wasn't listening. Now his thumb and forefinger tweaked a nipple between them and her eyes nearly rolled up in her head. She had to do something now before things really got out of control. She kissed his temple in apology, then yanked on his hair as hard as she could.

"Ouch! Hell, woman, what are you doing?" Ray let her go and stumbled backwards, rubbing his head.

"I'm sorry." She touched his cheek. "We had to stop, Ray, don't you see?"

His pupils were dilated and his skin flushed beneath his day's growth of whiskers. She could clearly see his engorged shaft beneath his pants. Her pulse thrummed through her and the ache between her legs howled in hunger.

"You didn't have to pull my hair," he muttered.

"It was better than kicking you...well, you know...*there*."

His eyebrows shot up. "I'm surprised you know where."

She shrugged. "I've had to protect myself. I didn't really want to hurt you, Ray. I...I'm confused but I would never want to do anything to hurt you."

He nodded. "I know that. I'm...sorry I went so fast. I didn't intend... Dammit. I can't seem to control myself around you."

"I know the feeling," Lily said. And meant every word. Even now, she was having trouble not dragging him to her bedroom to finish what they started. Her body positively pulsed with desire, with unrequited passion. It would be a long time before either one of them slept that night.

CR SO

Ray insisted on staying home for another two days before they left. There were things he needed to do. Melody refused to leave without her Pa, so they all waited. Trevor and Brett hung around to escort them, much to Ray's apparent annoyance.

Lily was nervous about meeting the rest of Ray's family, but determined she would do her best not to embarrass herself. It might be inevitable; however, she would strive as hard as she could. Her body purred whenever Ray was around, like a lovesick puppy whining for its master. Lily tried to keep her distance from Ray, but it was impossible.

When they sat for dinner, his gaze strayed to hers, nearly singeing holes in her clothes. He seemed just as miserable and frustrated as she was. Soon that particular dam was going to overflow.

It was Thursday afternoon and Melody hid in the house somewhere. She heard Melody humming "Twinkle Twinkle Little Star". Lily was just heading into the pantry, where the noise was the loudest, when a knock came at the door.

"Dammit!" Lily cursed, then stomped her foot. "I cannot believe I said that."

She walked to the door, smoothing her hair and trying to calm her frayed nerves. She opened it to find three unfamiliar women on the porch. They were of varying ages, but were dressed similarly in dark blue and gray with big wool capes and fancy mufflers.

"Good afternoon. May I help you?"

"Oh, she's so polite and well-spoken. I knew it," the short, plump one offered. She had rosy cheeks and dark brown hair.

"Yes, yes, you're always right." The tall, thin one had graying hair and a hawk-like nose.

"Stop it, you two. You're scaring her," said the youngest of the three, with blonde hair and beautiful blue eyes. She held out one white-gloved hand. "Hello, I'm Elizabeth Goodson."

Lily was at a loss for words. Who were these three women?

"I'm Beatrice Kincaid," the plump one introduced herself.

"And I am Edwina Malficent," the tall one uttered with a sniff.

"We're from Cheshire and we've come to welcome you to town." Elizabeth smiled.

Lily returned the smile. "That's wonderful. Please come in."

She ushered them inside, then took their cloaks, bonnets, mufflers and gloves to lay on her bed, praying she wouldn't trip, rip or destroy anything along the way. After dropping the load on the bed, she smoothed her hair again and returned to her guests. Never had she been visited by a welcome committee before.

She walked into the living room to find the three women whispering pointedly. They all stopped and turned toward her.

"I'll go make some tea for us." Lily escaped to the kitchen.

They made her nervous, no doubt about that. She fumbled a bit with the stove, but finally got the flames burning brightly. Her cheeks flushed and her heart had taken up residence halfway up her throat. After making the tea, she carefully arranged everything on a tray with some fresh cookies, and went back into the living room.

Again the three of them were in a tête-à-tête that excluded her.

"That looks lovely, Miss Wickham," Beatrice said politely.

"Very lovely," echoed Elizabeth.

Edwina just humphed. Somehow an angel was riding on Lily's shoulder because she set the tray down and successfully poured the tea without spilling, breaking or dropping anything.

As they sipped their tea, they spoke of the weather and how cold it was compared to New York. The conversation was odd, stilted. Something was amiss with these visitors, but Lily didn't know what and her internal alarms clanged noisily. Lily waited for the proverbial other shoe to drop.

Elizabeth wiped her mouth with a napkin and set her teacup on the tray. "That was very nice, Miss Wickham. Thank you. After I spoke with my mother in the general store, I knew we had to come out and welcome you."

Lily waited.

"And to warn you," Elizabeth continued.

"Yes, definitely warn you," chimed in Beatrice.

"That is an evil, hateful man you are working for," Edwina proclaimed. "He has sinned in the eyes of God and this town. He continues to harbor a bastard half-breed child and thumb his nose at society. Mark my words, he will bring you down to the depths of Hades to which he has sunk."

Lily was absolutely speechless. She'd known something was amiss, but hadn't expected this.

"We would like to offer you a job as a school teacher in Cheshire." Elizabeth's tone was cajoling but insistent. "There is a position open and it includes living with my family in town. The pay is only fifteen dollars a month, but we would treat you as one of our own."

"Yes, yes, one of our own." Beatrice apparently enjoyed repeating things like a parrot.

"The most important thing is to get you away from that man before he forces himself on you," Edwina said with a firm nod.

Lily knew her response to these women was important. What she wanted to do was boot them on their bustled behinds out the door. She also wanted Melody to be able to hold her head high in town and small-minded thinkers must always be tolerated or they could make life a living hell.

"I don't know what to say to all this, ladies. Mr. Malloy has been the kindest employer I could ask for. He has done nothing untoward nor has he acted like a devil. Melody is a wonderful child and I enjoy teaching her. While your offer is most kind, I prefer to stay on the Double R Ranch, particularly since I signed a contract to do so."

There, take that.

Elizabeth's blue eyes grew cold and hard as she listened to Lily. "You will regret staying here. My sister couldn't stay under his thumb, especially after he presented his Indian bastard in place of her stillborn daughter."

Now Lily was shocked. What in the world was Elizabeth talking about?

"Mark my words, Miss Wickham, Raymond Malloy will stop at nothing to get what he wants from women. Then discard them like broken dolls."

Lily couldn't help the traitorous shiver that snaked up her spine at the fervor in Elizabeth's voice or the fire in her eyes. She acted like a woman scorned.

"I-I appreciate your assistance, but I will stay."

With more dire warnings as they suited up to return to town, the three of them left the house like the three witches of Macbeth. Leaving trouble brewing in their wake.

ରଃ ৪০

Ray could tell something was wrong with Lily. She wasn't her usual smiling self. In fact, during dinner, he swore she scowled at him, but when he turned to look, her glance darted away. Trevor kept up his ever-present chatter and Brett remained as quiet as a stone.

"Some witches came to the house today," said Melody.

Lily's mouth dropped open. "Melody."

"It's true." Melody talked around a piece of bread in her mouth. "I heard you say they was witches after they left. They also said bad things about my Pa and about me."

Lily looked as if she didn't know whether to paddle her fanny or hug her for finally talking to her.

"What witches?" Ray asked Lily.

She frowned at Melody. "They weren't witches. They were a welcoming committee from town."

Melody snorted just like her father. Trevor snickered.

"Who were they?" Ray demanded.

His heart thumped and his palms grew damp. He had a feeling he was not going to like the answer.

"I don't remember their names," Lily said, her eyes dropping to her plate. Using her fork, she toyed with the ham.

"I do. Beatrice somebody, Elizabeth Goodson and Edwin Mali-something. They were mean and told Lily awful things," supplied Melody.

"You don't talk for three weeks and now you decide to tattle. Melody Malloy, I hope you're good and ready to start your lessons." Lily appeared exasperated.

Ray's heart clenched and a river of fury coursed through him. It was worse than he thought. "Elizabeth Goodson was in *this* house? That bitch had the balls to walk through my door?" His voice rose as his anger washed over him. "I can't believe you let her in my fucking house."

Time seemed to stand still for a moment as every sound in the house was swallowed by the bellow of his fury. Lily looked truly frightened and Melody took off like a scampering mouse. He sensed his brothers staring at him hard.

"I…I didn't know who they were," Lily stuttered. "They showed up here and—"

"You do not let anyone in *my* house without my permission! She isn't worth the air that she breathes or the ground she slithers on. She is *not* to be let in this house. As for Beatrice, she's a moron, and Edwina Malficent is an obnoxious old crone who likes to throw hell at people."

Lily's mouth opened and closed without making a sound.

"Do you understand me?"

Lily nodded, then pushed her chair back and stood. "Excuse me."

She turned and left the room quietly.

"Jesus, Ray, you didn't have to flay her hide. She probably doesn't know anything about the Goodsons or what people in town to avoid. Have you told her?"

"Shut up, Trevor. It's none of your business."

Brett wiped his mouth with his napkin. "You were a mite harsh, Ray. You might want to apologize to Lillian. From what Mel said, they weren't very nice to her."

Brett didn't speak much, but when he did, Ray listened. His temper seemed to have a mind of its own and took off at will. He did yell at Lily and it wasn't her fault.

God, he hated apologizing as much as he hated talking about his feelings.

ᏯᎡ ᏰᎠ

Lily sat on her bed and blinked back tears. She wasn't going to cry over Ray yelling at her. She ought to be used to it. Ray's favorite method of talking was yelling. But it still hurt. She didn't do anything wrong intentionally. Obviously Elizabeth was well-known to Ray, and intensely disliked.

She sat there staring out through the window into the inky night until someone knocked softly at the door.

"Yes?"

"It's Ray. Can I come in?"

She had never heard him knock before. Should she be nervous or impressed?

"Come in," she called out.

The door opened slowly and Ray's bulk filled the doorway. For a moment, he was nothing but dark shadows, then he came into the light thrown by the lantern. He had his hands in his pockets and was looking at the floor. She had never expected to see a repentant Ray.

"I came to say I'm sorry. It ain't easy for me. I reckon I've said it less than half a dozen times in my life. Trevor about knocked my ass in the ground for yelling at you."

"I didn't know who they were. I didn't mean—"

"I know you didn't. I acted like a horse's ass. Those three have been treating me and mine like shit for five years and I'm sick of it. This was the first time they came to my house though and it really rankled me."

"I'm sorry."

He shook his head. "You don't need to be sorry. I'm the one who came to apologize."

Her heart felt immeasurably lighter than it had for hours. "Thank you, Ray. I accept your apology."

He raised his head and looked at her. The current between them was strong enough to make the hairs on her arms stand up. Tired of fighting the rapids, she decided to throw herself into them, to get carried away downstream. Lily stood and walked over to Ray. She reached behind him and closed the door, locking it. The sound of the key turning in the tumblers was loud in the quiet room; the only other sound was the fire crackling and their breathing.

"What are you doing, Lily?"

She came up behind him and laid her palms flat on his back. He was warm, nearly hot to the touch, and so very firm. His breath hitched as she explored his marvelously wide back.

"I can't sleep anymore, Ray. Dreams of you are tormenting me."

He made a sound like he was choking, then cleared his throat. "Tormenting you?"

Her hands barely reached above his shoulders, but she continued to caress him, including the incredibly soft hairs curling around the nape of his neck.

"Mmm hmmm. I can't get rest because of it. You started this and I want to finish it."

She walked around the front of him, trailing her hands down his arm, then across his gorgeous chest.

"Jesus, Lily, what are you doing?"

She looked up and when brown met green, the decision was completely made. She cupped his face in her small hands and brought his lips down to hers.

Yes.

It was what she needed. What she desired. At that moment, she didn't care if she went to hell. It was worth it. He resisted at first, but she nibbled and kissed until he groaned and swept her up into his arms. His hardness pressing into her softness. Like the key in the lock.

Perfect.

Ray pulled her body to him tightly. His hard arousal pushed against her throbbing pussy, making her gasp with pleasure as heat flowed between them. Her pulse pounded through her veins like a primal drumbeat.

Yes.

"Please, Ray…"

Lily started yanking at his shirt, but it remained tucked into his pants.

"Help me."

He moved away from her lips for a moment to wrench his shirt over his head. She saw a magnificent blend of muscle and reddish-brown chest hair, muscle and sinew together as perfectly as God intended.

"Now you," he murmured as he claimed her lips again. His tongue darted inside her mouth as he deftly unbuttoned her dress until it pooled around her waist. With one shove, it landed on the floor along with her petticoats. His hands crept down to the bottom of her chemise and slowly lifted it up. The cool air hit her breasts and her nipples grew even harder, peaked with ripeness and hunger.

Yes.

He broke the kiss again and stepped back to pull her chemise off. Naked except for her stockings, she felt the sudden urge to cover herself. Her hands drifted toward her breasts and Ray growled, a sound that made Lily shiver as she dampened in excitement.

"Don't you dare."

He cupped her more-than-ample breasts. She closed her eyes and gloried in his calloused fingers pinching, caressing and plucking her sensitive nipples. With each touch, an answering tug sounded between her legs, and the ache within her intensified.

Lily couldn't stop herself from exploring his chest and stomach, feeling the wiry hairs beneath her fingers. She dipped lower toward his waistband just as his hand landed between her legs. Her pussy clenched with want as he cupped her and she squeezed his hardened cock. They both sucked in an audible breath. Time stood still as their eyes met.

"Are you ready for this, Lily?"

"Yes, yes and yes. Please don't tell me you're going to stop."

"Only if I want to kill myself." Ray laughed hoarsely. "I can't fight this anymore, Lily. I…just can't."

She fumbled with his buttons until he took pity on her. In a blink, he flipped them open and shimmied off his pants and long underwear. Lily had seen naked men before, but Ray put them to shame. He was perfectly formed, even generously formed. Wide shoulders graced with layers of bronzed muscle followed by long arms that seemed sculpted from warm granite. His chest led down to a nicely formed belly then to his cock, which stood at attention, pulsing and hungry, cupped by a pair of balls and a nest of brown hair. His legs were long, tapering to a pair of feet that seemed larger than average. He had scars, too many scars, but they appeared a natural part of Ray—he was a man marked by scars inside and out.

For now, this here and now, he was hers. She reached out and stroked him. His cock was long and smooth, hard and pulsing. She closed her eyes and imagined this was the first of a lifetime of loving with him.

He swooped down to kiss her with a ferocity she hadn't felt yet. His hand crept between her legs again and began to rub back and forth. The pleasure zinged through her as she grew wetter and swollen against his fingers. She needed more, she needed him.

"Like roses and petals," he said.

"Like steel and satin," she replied.

She felt him smile against her lips and wished like heck she could have *seen* him smile.

Ray slowly started backing her toward the bed. When her legs hit the mattress, he picked her up and sat her on the edge. His hands pushed her thighs open so he could nestle between them. The first time his cock touched her hot flesh, she moaned in tune with him as desire sang through her veins.

Yes.

He rubbed himself in her wet pussy, the friction and heat driving her to distraction. Her body clenched, needing him, wanting him.

"Please…" she whispered.

Ray grabbed her mouth in a profound, soul-wrenching kiss as he pushed himself inside her inch by inch. She stretched to accommodate him, her body overcome with pulsing need. When he was fully sheathed, tears pricked her lids from the sheer perfection of having him inside her. It was more than just sex—it was heaven.

He began to thrust in and out as one hand caressed and tantalized her breast, the other stroked her nubbin of pleasure. Bolts of pleasure shot through her, making her legs twitch as she struggled to maintain control of her body. Her legs wrapped around his back and he plunged over and over, deeper and deeper, touching her womb and her heart.

Yes.

"Lily," he whispered harshly. "Sweet Lily."

His tempo increased until he nearly pounded her. She met his thrusts with her own, faster, harder. The coil within her pulled up tighter and tighter as she reached for a pinnacle she'd never seen before. He released her mouth and took a gasping breath.

"Come for me, baby," he said.

While she exploded into a thousand pieces, he said her name again and again as he plunged in so far he touched her soul. Stars swirled around her body, twinkling and bursting into small flames. She clenched around him so tightly they became one. It was as if the heavens had come to earth and taken up residence in her heart.

Lily clutched Ray to her, his sweaty chest pressed into her cheek. She held onto her happiness like the fleeting bit of life it was.

"Jesus, Lily. I didn't…"

"Neither did I," she replied.

He slowly withdrew and stepped away from her. She closed her legs and looked up into his eyes. The green was almost gone his pupils were so large. He was covered in a sheen of sweat, his mouth soft and swollen from kissing her.

"I never meant for that to happen."

"It was going to happen anyway."

He swept his hand through his wavy hair, making the curls stick up every which way. Making him look boyish. Making her fall more in love with him.

He grabbed his clothes and dressed quickly. Lily stood and picked up her chemise, somehow getting herself tangled enough that he tsked and rescued her. When he pulled it down over her shoulders, she was nearly brought to her knees by the sight of Ray's smile.

Lord in Heaven, he was *stunning*.

Lily slipped along in the rapids, heading toward the waterfall. It was inevitable. She was falling so fast, there was no way to stop it.

CR SO

Ray walked to his room in a daze. His body hummed with heat and sexual satisfaction. Never, *never* in his life had he been so completely stunned by sex. Stunned. That was the word for it.

Stunned.

It had been more than five years since he'd had sex, so it was inevitable that the first time he did, there would be a big release. He hadn't expected it to change his life. But it did. Lily did.

She was truthful—she was no virgin. Thank God. He didn't think he could've held back any of the passion that clambered to get out. Especially after he saw how perfect she was. Large breasts topped with the palest pink nipples, narrow waist, generous hips, and the ability to send him to the stars.

He was turning the doorknob when he sensed he was being watched. He glanced over at Melody's door. She peered out at him with her old-soul eyes.

"You were in Miss Wickham's room."

Damn. This kid missed nothing.

"Yes I was. I had to apologize for being rude to her," he said as he squatted down to her eye level. "Just like I owe you an apology. I'm sorry I yelled at you, Little Note."

She continued to hide behind the door. "It's okay. I know you weren't mad at me. You were mad at the witches and Miss Wickham."

Ray shook his head. How could he make her understand? The three women who made their lives a living hell in town had the brass balls to walk through his door like they were paying a social visit. He was sure they had spewed lies to Lily. Thank God she had a good head on her shoulders.

"I'm not mad at Lily, honey. She didn't do anything wrong."

"Those witches said bad things about you, Pa."

There was a little hitch in her voice, but she didn't come to him.

"I know. They won't be back, I promise."

Damn straight. He'd shoot those cows in the ass if they even stepped foot on his land.

"Okay. Goodnight, Pa."

"Do you want me to tuck you in?"

"No, Uncle Trevor already did. He held my ears while we walked down the hallway too. I told him to stop, but he didn't."

Ray felt his cheeks flush.

Shit.

"I'm sorry I missed it. Tomorrow I'll tuck you in twice."

She rolled her eyes and shook her head. "You're silly, Pa. Goodnight."

"Goodnight, Mel."

She closed the door and Ray stared at the floor beneath his feet for a moment before he stood. The day had been the strangest and most incredible at the same time. One thing was certain, he would never be the same person again.

CHAPTER EIGHT

They were finally headed for the Malloy family ranch. With help from Trevor and Brett, they loaded the wagon with what they'd need for two days. Ray tied his horse, Shadow, to the back. He was a beautiful, huge gray beast with soulful eyes. Lily didn't normally take to horses, but this one seemed special.

As Ray tucked Melody in the back with some blankets, Lily looked up at the beautiful blue skies overhead. It would be an uneventful trip and Ray said it would only take two hours. Apparently the land the Double R sat on was a gift to Ray and his ex-wife when they got married. She stepped forward to get in the wagon and apparently found a piece of ice, because her feet went out from under her and she landed on her back. All the air whooshed out of her body and her head smacked the ground painfully.

"Jesus, Lily. Are you okay?" Trevor exclaimed.

"What happened? Is she all right?" Brett chimed in.

"Would you both shut up?" Ray knelt beside her. With a small shake of his head, he helped her sit up. "Anything broken?"

"I don't think so." She pressed her mittened hand to her throbbing head. "But I think I'm going to have a headache.

She winced as Ray pulled her to her feet. He brushed the snow off the back of her coat.

"We've got to stop meeting when you're lying in the snow," he murmured.

She smiled. "Maybe we can meet someplace else instead."

She could not believe she said that. Apparently neither could he from the surprise in his eyes. He reached out one finger and wiped something off her cheek. His skin was rough and calloused, sending a shiver of pleasure straight down her body to her mons.

Someone, probably Trevor, cleared his throat, breaking the spell that had fallen over Lily and Ray. His eyes were a combination of confusion, arousal and, dare she think it, happiness.

Lily's heart did a leap the likes of which it had never done before. She imagined it had been some time since happiness had taken residence in Ray's life. She was happy to be witness to its return.

"Ready?" he asked.

She nodded and he took her elbow to guide her to the wagon. After helping her on board, he jumped up and grabbed the reins. Lily shifted on the hard wooden seat. She was a bit tender and felt herself blush at the reason why.

With very little fanfare, the small party was off to the Malloy family ranch. Lily tried to tell the butterflies in her stomach to shoo, but they continued to flutter.

Lily was nervous about meeting the rest of the family. Would they know what she and Ray had been doing? Would they approve? She was supposed to be a governess and teacher for a five-year-old girl. Instead she was a housekeeper and mistress.

The butterflies were joined by a pack of moths, and perhaps a flock of birds.

CR SO

They had been traveling for half an hour when Lily realized the bitter cold was seeping through her layers of wool and penetrating her down to the bone. She was still not used to such freezing temperatures. She couldn't feel her nose anymore and her cheeks were so tight, she was afraid they'd crack if she smiled. She clenched her jaw to keep her teeth from chattering. Unfortunately, that didn't stop the shivering.

"Are you cold, Lily?"

Lily refused to admit it. He would think she wasn't tough enough to last in the Wyoming climate.

"No, I'm fine."

"Your knees are knocking louder than the horses' hooves. Why don't you climb in back with Melody and get under the blankets."

That sounded wonderful. Her shivering body reacted to the invitation and shudders joined the shivers.

"Melody, would it be all right if I came back there and shared those warm blankets?" Lily thought she should ask the girl to give her the option to say no.

A muffled reply came from the back. "It's okay."

Ray pulled the wagon to a stop and held her hand while she climbed over the seat into the back. Melody was hunkered down between two crates, a blanket beneath her and three on top, with a quilt wrapped around.

"You look like a caterpillar," Lily said as she squeezed in next to Melody and arranged the blankets around them. "Ohh, it's nice and warm in here."

The combination of Melody's body warmth with hers and the warm wool blankets was just delightful.

"Yup."

Ray started riding again after Lily was settled. In minutes, the shivers and shudders had receded and she felt warm.

"Thank you so much, Melody."

"'Kay."

Lily shifted and felt something hard pressing into her hip. After a minute, she realized it was a book.

"Did you bring your McGuffey's Reader?"

Melody nodded.

"Would you like to work on your letters and sounds again? You did so well at the store with the list."

She didn't answer, but Lily felt Melody's little body tense up. What was she afraid of?

"I dunno."

"I know a song about the alphabet. Would you like to learn it?"

Melody hesitated. "Okay."

Lily started singing.

CR SO

Ray listened to Lily quietly singing with his daughter in the crisp morning air on his way to his parents' house, with two of his brothers riding ahead of him. He searched for the right word for what he was feeling. It was contentment. *Contentment.*

Life had kicked him in the balls so many times, he'd forgotten what contentment felt like. Smiles and laughter were not part of his daily routine. Ray felt a jolt of shock to realize how much he'd been missing. He didn't know if he was ready to open his arms and let the world come on in, but one voluptuous brunette was knocking down his walls piece by piece. If he wasn't careful, she'd be inside his heart and he'd never be able to let her go.

Within another hour, he arrived at the Malloy family ranch. The ranch house had stood for nearly forty years. John Malloy built it with his two hands after he and his wife, Francesca, settled there back in 1852. A year later, Ray was born, and the house sheltered, protected and served as a beacon for all to return to. It was a home.

Ray felt his chest lighten as they pulled into the yard. The door swung open and his brothers, Jack and Ethan, came out in a rush.

"Thank God you're here, Mama is about to drive us all insane," Jack exclaimed with his usual drama.

Jack was the youngest of the Malloy brothers at twenty-nine. He'd been married for nearly five years to the love of his life, Rebecca. They had an eight-year-old adopted daughter named Hope, a four-year-old son named Gideon and a two-year-old son named Malcolm.

Ethan was the second oldest Malloy brother. He had been married for ten years to his wife, Bonita. They had no children, but they spoiled their nieces and nephews rotten. He had the same wavy brown hair and blue eyes as Jack.

Together they looked like twins, separated by eight years of age. Their harried looks suggested they'd been wrestling bears, with hair that had been pulled at more than once.

Trevor chuckled as he dismounted.

"It's not funny, Trevor. Where the hell have you been?" said Ethan with a frown.

"I had things to take care of at the Double R," Ray answered. "Trev and Brett stayed to help." He cocked one eyebrow at them, daring them to contradict him. They only smiled.

Ray set the brake and wrapped the reins around the lever. He hopped down into the snow and shook hands with Jack and Ethan.

"Things? We've been here and you wouldn't believe what the kids have been up to. Malcolm is reminding me of his namesake. I think he stole Hope's journal. And the twins. What is Nicky feeding them? I swear I—"

"Jack, shut up for a minute, would you? Say hello to Lily. Ethan, I'd like you to meet Miss Wickham."

Jack's eyes widened and he smiled at Lily, who looked over the side of the wagon with a grin on her face.

"Hello, Jack. It's wonderful to see you again."

"Hi, Lily. Forget everything I just said. The children are behaving like angels. I swear."

She shook her head and laughed. "I'm sure they are. Melody has been the perfect traveler."

"Mel!" cried Jack as he reached in the wagon and plucked her out. She squealed as he threw her over his shoulder and headed back for the house.

"I got what I came for." Jack laughed.

Melody giggled and waved as she disappeared into the house.

"It's nice to meet you, Ethan," Lily offered politely.

He smiled and held out his hands to help her down. "Good morning, Miss Wickham. I've heard a lot about you from Nicky and Tyler."

Ray felt a clench of something—was it jealousy?—deep down in his gut. He elbowed Ethan out of the way.

"Don't you have to go find Bonita or something?" he said with more than a hint of grumpiness.

Ethan laughed and his eyebrows went up. Ray saw a sparkle in his brother's blue eyes that foretold of some ribbing later on.

Shit.

It was worth it when Lily leaned into his hands and he was able to touch her again. The clench immediately lessened and disappeared completely when she smiled at him with her rosy cheeks and pink-tipped nose.

In fact, he felt something radically different. Something he didn't even recognize at all. It scared the hell out of him.

ଔ ଏ

The Malloys were simply overwhelming. From a girl who lived the first eleven years of her life with the dregs of humanity, and another ten in an orphanage, that was saying a lot.

Lily greeted them all by bumping into Ray's mother who then bumped into Ray's father and knocked over the table beside the door. The table landed with a crash, scaring the children who in turn started screeching and crying.

Lily gazed at everyone apologetically but with more than a bit of horror.

Ray's father, who looked very much like an older version of Ray, started chuckling, that turned into a guffaw as he helped his wife to stand. By then Francesca was laughing, and then everyone was laughing. Lily felt two inches tall and wished she could climb back in the wagon and drive to New York.

"Well, Miss Lily," said Ray's father as he wiped his eyes. "I'm John Malloy. Welcome to our family. You'll fit in just fine around here."

His eyes twinkled merrily and she saw him swallowing back more laughter. Ray's mother elbowed him out of the way.

"Move over, John." She had a slight French accent and warm eyes. She looked a lot like Nicky with her curly brownish-red hair and green eyes; however, she stood a good six inches shorter. Much closer to Lily's own height. Thank God she wasn't the only petite woman in the house.

"I'm Francesca. Welcome, *cheri.*"

She folded Lily into a hug that banished her fear and embarrassment in a wink. Francesca smelled of roses and bread and cinnamon. Lily's eyes pricked as she was hugged, *truly hugged,* for the first time in her life.

"Thank you, Francesca," she managed to croak.

From then on, Lily was introduced to the rest of the family and children. There were so many of them, and they all seemed to love each other, and to love to tease each other. Lily watched them, fascinated by the closeness, the camaraderie. It was like going to the theatre and watching a play. This is what she'd been missing all her life. A family.

The men all went off to do something manly and the women converged in the kitchen, drinking tea and eating scrumptious slabs of homemade bread with honey. Lily sat at the table with Nicky, Rebecca, Bonita and Francesca. The children napped and played quietly.

Rebecca was Jack's wife. A beautiful blonde with enormous gray eyes reflecting a soul that had traveled a hard path and was grateful to be happy and in love with her husband. Lily felt an immediate kinship to Rebecca, who also hugged her when they met.

Nicky was dressed in trousers again. Lily wondered if she ever wore dresses, but doubted it.

Bonita was just that, beautiful. She seemed to be part Indian or perhaps part Mexican, Lily wasn't sure. She was very quiet and had an innate grace and dignity about her that spoke volumes. She was a few inches taller than Lily with long, straight black hair, dark chocolate eyes and mocha-colored skin. She wore a colorful turquoise blouse with a black flowing skirt. Her jewelry was also turquoise and she shyly admitted she had made it herself.

Francesca was a strong woman who ordered the men around like a little general. And they obeyed her immediately. She took Lily under her wing and kept her by her side the entire morning and afternoon. Now Francesca sat beside Lily at the table, lending her unspoken support to the fish out of water.

Rebecca nibbled daintily on a piece of bread and sipped her tea. Lily hoped one day she could be as graceful and composed as Rebecca.

"Wyoming must be a bit colder than New York," Rebecca mused.

Lily laughed, recalling how cold she'd been in the wagon on the way over. She was so thankful to be toasty warm in the Malloy ranch house.

"A bit. Okay, a lot. I'm getting used to it though."

Nicky nodded. "I was away for three years and coming back was a slap in the face, literally, with cold. It's the kind of cold that bites you."

There was a moment of silence while everyone concentrated on tea and bread.

"Have you lived in New York all your life?" asked Nicky as she slathered another piece of bread with honey.

"No, I, uh…traveled quite a bit when I was young with my parents. I started living in New York when I arrived at St. Catherine's orphanage in Queens."

"Oh, really, where did you travel?"

Lily dreaded the question, but didn't want to lie about where she'd lived.

"Here and there. Lots of places. My father liked to gamble and my mother was a singer."

Nicky nodded. "Met lots of folks like that when I was on the run."

Lily was immediately intrigued. "On the run?" She could have kicked herself for asking it. It just popped out of her mouth.

Nicky laughed at the expression on her face. "Don't be embarrassed. I was on the run from bounty hunters and the law for over three years for a crime I didn't commit. Tyler found me, married me, dragged me back here to face the music. In the end, the man who caused us a lot of suffering," she glanced at Rebecca, "got the punishment he deserved."

"Is Tyler a bounty hunter?" Lily's mouth didn't seem to want to stop moving.

"He was—not anymore. He was really good at it too. After all, he found me, didn't he?" Nicky grinned.

The conversation turned to springtime and waiting for the thaw to happen. Lily felt so comfortable sitting and talking to them. They were like the sisters, and the mother, she'd never had. She felt a roar of envy building inside her. What she wouldn't give to be a part of them permanently.

"How are the lessons going with Melody?" Francesca asked.

Lily choked on her tea and nearly aspirated it. Nicky started slapping her on the back as Lily struggled for breath. As she wiped her eyes on a napkin, she coughed and cleared her throat.

"That bad, huh?" Nicky said.

"Melody likes to…to hide. I'm still learning how to find her."

Nicky laughed, as did Francesca. Bonita and Rebecca looked as puzzled as Lily.

"My daughter was the champion hider in her day. Her brothers could never find her." Francesca smiled.

"She is resisting you?" Rebecca's delicate brow puckered.

Lily nodded. "She loves music though. I think that's where I am going to try to break through. If her father doesn't continue to fight me on it."

"Why would he do that?" Francesca frowned.

Nicky glanced at her mother. "The piano, Mama. It's still there."

Francesca face hardened and her lips compressed together to form a white line. "He keeps punishing himself for that faithless woman's ugly decisions."

"Yup, he sure does." Nicky pointed at Lily. "But I have a feeling that Lily here is the perfect cure for what ails him."

Lily felt her cheeks redden. "Wh-what do you mean?"

"I saw the way you look at Ray, and I also saw him *smile* at you earlier." Nicky's grin was positively wicked.

Francesca, Bonita and Rebecca gasped. If she wasn't so embarrassed, she might laugh at the comic expressions on their faces.

"He *smiled*? At Lily?" Francesca sounded incredulous.

Nicky smiled smugly and raised an eyebrow at Lily. "Damn straight he did. I think Ray has fallen for his governess. I also think that the feeling might be mutual."

Lily gazed at the women around the table, waiting for the recriminations, the accusations and the disapproval. Instead, she saw excitement, joy, approval and, best of all, acceptance.

"You will be good for Raymond," stated Francesca. "He needs a good woman and if you can make him smile, Lily, you are definitely the one. I knew my friend, Agatha, would find the perfect governess."

She leaned over and kissed Lily on both cheeks then hugged her tightly. "Welcome to the family, daughter."

CHAPTER NINE

Lily woke with a start, her heart pounding and her breath coming in gasps. It had been so long since she had that particular nightmare, she had all but forgotten it. Almost. Briefly talking about where she'd lived and her parents was enough to wake it from its slumber.

It was always the same dream. Reliving the last day with her parents. The awful bar, the smelly men, the panic and the fear. Then the tears and the pain.

Enough.

She shook off the self-pity, wiped the tears from her cheeks and swung her legs over the side of the bed, careful not to wake Hope. Lily shared a bed with Rebecca's eight-year-old daughter, Hope. She was a little version of her mother right down to the soulful gray eyes. A beautiful, smart child who read a bedtime story to the rest of the children, then helped tuck them in. Melody and little Rebecca slept on cots on the other side of the room. All three girls slept soundly.

Lily tiptoed across the room with her bathrobe in hand. She slipped it on after she got out to the hallway and closed the door.

As she headed to the kitchen for some warm milk, she repressed the urge to review all the things Nicky and Francesca said about her and Ray. It was too much to hope for, too much to ask for; however, that didn't stop her traitorous heart from galloping at the thought of Ray loving her.

The kitchen and dining room at the Malloy ranch were one big room, "the great room" their mother called it. It was an open, airy place that still maintained its coziness. A warm glow of light came from the room. Someone else was awake.

CR SO

Ray stared at the whiskey in his glass as he rolled it back and forth between his hands. It was his third and he shouldn't even be thinking about drinking it, much less have it already poured, but he was. Because of her.

Lily.

The very thought of her made his dick wake up and stretch. As he watched his parents, then Nicky and Tyler, then Ethan and Bonita, and finally Jack and Rebecca all happily head off to bed together, his longing for Lily intensified. He hungered for her, ached for her. Yet he had to share a room with Trevor and Brett, he thought sourly. What he wanted to do was throw her over his shoulder and carry her off to bed and damn the consequences.

He couldn't do that to her though. His family obviously liked and respected her. He didn't want to jeopardize that by acting like a caveman making off with his woman.

His woman.

Was she? He wasn't the first to be in Lily's bed, a fact that didn't bother him. Was he going to be the last? He jumped at the *yes* his heart shouted at him.

His woman.

People didn't fall in love in three weeks, did they? He had been unhappily living his life with no warmth or hope. Then came Lily, tripping into his life with her amazing outlook on life.

"Hello, Ray."

As if his imagination conjured her, she appeared in the doorway. He started and spilled his whiskey all over his hands. Her hair hung down in a thick braid he itched to unravel and press against him. Her nightclothes were modest and covered her completely, but he saw her curves and bountiful breasts. His hands shook with the urge to cup them, weigh them and bring them to his waiting mouth.

"Oh, I'm sorry." Lily hurried to the sink to grab the towel hanging on the side. As she stepped over to him to wipe his hands, he was assaulted by her scent. She smelled of wildflowers and soap and woman.

His hunger grew teeth and starting gnawing on him.

"What are you doing here?" His question was gruff even to his own ears.

"I'm sorry I disturbed you," she said as she set the towel down. Her cheeks were pink and her beautiful whiskey eyes reflected hurt. She turned to leave and he grabbed her arm. He tugged and she tumbled into his lap with a squeak. He closed his eyes for a moment to savor the intense wave of pleasure zinging through him as her soft bottom cushioned his growing erection and her right breast pushed against his chest.

He opened his eyes and looked at her. Her mouth was slightly parted and her eyes wide.

"I missed you."

He didn't really mean to say it even if that's what he was thinking.

She smiled and wrapped her arms around his neck. "I missed you too."

"I can't help it, Lily," he said as he swooped down to kiss her.

Her lips welcomed his and immediately began to move with him. Long, slow kisses with tongues sliding against each other, a dance of thirst that had not yet been slaked. A hunger not fed.

Ray felt her nipple harden and grind into his chest. He was sure she could feel his dick pressing against her hip. It was as hard as a fence post. He wanted to rip her nightgown off and plunge into her. He *needed* her.

His hand started inching up her leg, caressing and touching the silky smooth flesh. As he got closer to her upper thigh, her hand closed around his wrist and she pulled her lips away from his.

"We can't do this in the kitchen, Ray. One of the children could walk in."

He groaned and rested his forehead against hers. His body throbbed in tune with the pulse in his pants. Now was not the time to stop the concert.

"Goddamn kids," he grumbled.

She turned down the wick in the lantern on the table next to them and started planting light kisses along his neck. "How…about…the…pantry?"

He didn't even think, he simply scooped her up and stood, heading for the pantry like a train on the tracks, with only one thought in his mind.

My woman.

As the room plunged into darkness, the muted moonlight streamed through the kitchen window. Ray pushed aside the curtain to the pantry and walked in with his precious bundle.

The pantry was large by some standards—at least eight feet deep and six feet wide. The Malloy family was eight strong before the youngest brother was killed nine years earlier. That was a lot of people, especially boys and men, to feed. He set Lily on a barrel and stepped away. It was nearly pitch black in there and only the white of her bathrobe was visible.

"Wait right there."

He rushed back into the kitchen, grabbed his coat from the hook beside the door and returned to the pantry in seconds. He handed her the coat, then lifted her up into his arms.

"Spread it on the barrel, sunshine."

Lily lay the coat inside up so the soft wool was beneath her. He set her down, sliding the nightgown up to her waist as he did. Leaning over, he licked her lips and whispered, "We've got to be quiet."

She nodded against him. Her braid bounced gently against his shoulder. He reached out and pulled the scrap of cloth off the end, then used his fingers to separate the strands. It felt like silk and he wanted it wrapped around him when he entered her.

Her small hands flattened against his chest, gently kneading and touching. He yanked his shirt off with one swoop and threw it on the floor. When her fingers starting walking down his bare chest, he knew he had to get them both ready or he was going to lose control in his pants.

He untied the sash on her bathrobe and eased it off her shoulders, kissing the soft skin of her neck. She mewled like a kitten when he bit her earlobe. He licked it in apology.

"Move up a bit," Ray whispered.

Lily leaned forward and he lifted the hem of her nightdress up and over her head.

Naked. She was deliciously naked. He cupped her breasts, rubbing his thumbs back and forth across the puckered peaks. Her breath came in shorter spurts as she squirmed on the barrel. She finally reached for his trousers and he smiled into the darkness.

Leaning toward her, he captured her mouth in a soul-searing kiss he felt echo through his body. As he unbuttoned his pants and pushed them down, she clutched his shoulders and matched him kiss for kiss, lick for lick, suck for suck, nibble for nibble.

Ray left one hand on a breast and the other traveled down between her legs to her tantalizing pussy. She was so wet. His fingers slid back and forth, rubbing and teasing her. She bit his shoulder as he inserted one finger, then two inside her. Tight. She was so damn tight. She may not have been a virgin, but she sure as hell wasn't very experienced either.

His dick jumped as her hand encircled him, testing his length. Skitters of pleasure ricocheted up and down his spine.

"That's it, sunshine. Harder, faster. You won't hurt it, I promise."

She began moving faster, then surprised him by cupping his balls and squeezing lightly. They tightened up like walnuts and he knew he had to stop her before he came on her delicate fingers. He gently removed her hand, shushing her protests with a kiss that seemed to last for hours. Long, slow kisses, full of wet heat.

Ray knelt on the floor and spread her legs wide. He pulled her nether lips apart, then licked her in one long stroke from top to bottom. He breathed in her musky scent and his arousal heightened. *My woman.* She nearly jumped off the barrel onto a shelf with the pickles.

"Jesus Christ and his heavenly mother. What are you doing?" she hissed.

"Shhhhhh," he whispered. "Just let me pleasure you."

He felt her tense up and try to close her legs, but he didn't let her. No, ma'am. She wasn't going anywhere. Ray was determined to feast on her luscious juices. He eased two fingers inside her and proceeded to lick, kiss and nibble her clit. Her scent teased him while her taste coated his tongue. Delicious and sweet, he lapped at her wetness until she moaned.

"Oh my God," she said. "Ray, oh my God. I can't…it's…please."

When he put three fingers inside her heat and suckled her clit, she came like a tornado. Pulling his hair, squeezing his head with her thighs and convulsing around his hand so hard, he thought he heard his knuckles pop. He lapped at her until the tremors stopped. With one last, long lick, he stood and wrapped his arms around her.

He wasn't surprised to find her trembling, but he was surprised when she grabbed him and slammed herself up against his incredibly hard staff. His little governess was as hot as fire.

"I need you, Ray. Please."

His heart leapt along with the rest of him. No second request needed. He pulled her to the edge of the barrel and rubbed the head of his aching cock in her wetness.

"Oh, my, that feels good," she moaned.

Ray grunted in response. He couldn't possibly talk. After teasing both of them, he needed to be inside her. To become one with her. To find that lake of pleasure and peace. His eyes closed in pure ecstasy as he gently slid in. Heaven.

My woman.

He thrust in and out slowly, savoring every second, knowing they needed to hurry, but unable to. He wanted to grasp every last second of time and hold it as long as he could. The sounds of their flesh on flesh and her breath hitching was music to his ears. She was so tight, so fucking tight. Each time he slid in, he wanted to stay in. Forever.

He rolled her nipples between his fingers, pinching and tweaking them to turgid peaks. What he really wanted to do was suckle them, but the angle was all wrong. When she scraped her nails on his nipples, he slammed into her so hard, the barrel moved.

"Sorry," he chuckled. She surprised him constantly. He'd never expect a governess to play with his nipples, but it damn well felt amazing.

"Mmmm…again," she said in his ear as she nibbled the lobe.

It was the beginning of the end for him. The pleasure within him knew no bounds. He held onto her ass with both hands and started riding her. Faster and harder. The jars rattled a bit behind her. He didn't really give a shit.

"Yes! Ray, please… I'm almost…"

Her whispered plea broke the dam. He reached down and flicked her clit twice and she exploded around him, squeezing and milking him. The muscles of her cunt felt like an iron fist and he came so hard, he nearly pushed her completely off the barrel. Over and over, his body shook with pleasure as it coursed through him. He held her close as the pulses of bliss echoed. Their heartbeats thumped in the inky blackness.

"Lily, Lily, Lily," he said against her temple. His breathing was harsh, blowing strands of her hair around his face.

She kissed his cheek and leaned in closer.

"I feel like I've done something really stupid, Ray."

"Nah, this wasn't stupid." He ran his hand up and down her soft back. "This was heaven."

She leaned back and he tried to peer at her in the dark. All he saw was a bit of a reflection in her eyes and the soft outline of her face.

"Not this. I agree with you—it was heaven," she whispered softly. "I think I've fallen in love with you."

CR SO

Lily wished she could see his face, but it was too dark. She could, however, clearly feel him pull back. He quietly cleaned them both up with a neckerchief, then helped her into her nightgown and down from the barrel. After dressing, he held the curtain for her to go back into the kitchen, coat in hand.

He hadn't said a word since she confessed her love. Obviously he didn't return her love and didn't know how to turn her down gently. There wasn't anything gentle about Ray Malloy. So he did the next best thing. Nothing.

He let go of her arm by the table, then lit the lamp. The last she saw of him, he slipped on his coat and headed out the back door. Alone.

She was scared to death. Her body still pulsed with the pleasure they'd shared in the pantry, but the wood floor felt like ice under her feet. She started to shiver and it wasn't from cold. It was deeper than that.

Lily was afraid she had just given her love to a man who would never accept it, nor ever be able to return it.

CR SO

Ray stood on the porch, staring blindly into the darkness of the night. His body still hummed from another incredible sexual encounter that shook him down to his soul.

I think I've fallen in love with you.

He wasn't ready for that and he sure as hell wasn't expecting it. It hit him like a horse kick to the guts.

Jesus Christ on crutches!

He knew she was trouble, but he had no idea how much. He couldn't possibly ever return her love, but could he stay with her even knowing that? Would she want to be his mistress? Or, God forbid, his wife? He'd sworn never to marry again and here he was, talking to the stars about a woman who had gotten under his skin in three weeks. He didn't want to lose her, but he didn't want to keep her either.

He was thinking too much. Life tended to work itself out if you did nothing, didn't it? He snorted at his own stupidity. It didn't sound like a good idea. Lily would be expecting some kind of response, even if it was the one that hurt her irreparably.

Could he be with someone he could never trust? Would she accept him without that trust? Too many questions and the answers would only come when he talked to her.

Shit, he hated talking.

CHAPTER TEN

At breakfast the next morning, Trevor sat next to Lily and proceeded to turn on the charm. "Good morning, Miss Lily. You look just pretty as a picture with that yellow dress on." He set down coffee and a plate heaped with biscuits, bacon and eggs.

"Thank you, Trevor." She surreptitiously moved a little further down the bench from him.

Trevor was as handsome as any of the Malloys with a dazzling smile. He did not engender even a smidge of anything but appreciation for his good looks.

"You are most welcome," he said with a wink.

"Don't you have shit to do?" growled a familiar, grumpy voice from behind them.

"Raymond," Francesca called from the kitchen. "Did I just hear you curse?"

"No, Mama, it was Trevor."

"It sure as hell wasn't!" Trevor exclaimed with a frown.

Lily bit her lip to keep from smiling.

"Don't think I won't smack both your hands with a wooden spoon," warned Francesca.

"You're an ass," whispered Trevor.

"You're a fucking idiot," Ray whispered back.

Before she could blink, they were both hurrying out the door, grumbling and sniping at each other. They must be off to do some kind of manly cursing competition. She was alone at the table with a grin on her face.

She swore Ray was jealous of his brother. Jealous. That particular piece of information was like a chocolate cake. Rich, decadent and sweet. No man ever had cause to be jealous because of Lily before. The very idea that the man she loved was jealous made her heart sing with joy. Perhaps they had a chance after all.

CR ℅

The twins' birthday party was coming to an end. The younger children had already been put down for a nap. Nicky and Rebecca had gone to take a snooze with their little ones. Hope, Logan, little Rebecca and Melody were playing on the floor in the living room with Bonita and Ethan.

Lily helped Francesca clean up the kitchen. John sat at the table drinking coffee and nibbling on the last piece of cake.

"It was a good party, wasn't it, Fran?"

"Yes, it was. The twins loved their train whistles. Jack is so talented with wood."

Lily agreed. Jack made the table and chairs in the kitchen, as well as the rocking chair and half the furniture in the house. He wasn't only talented, he was gifted. Lily hoped to ask him to make something special for Melody but the time had gotten away from her. They were leaving in the morning to return to the Double R.

Before she could stop herself, the plate she was drying slipped out of her hands. Expecting a crash, she was surprised when it bounced instead.

"Tin plates," said Francesca as she bent to pick it up with her soapy hands. "Learned a long time ago to always use tin plates when there's children around."

Absurdly grateful for not being responsible for breaking yet another plate, Lily smiled. "Or a clumsy governess."

Francesca waved her hand, a few soapy bubbles flipping back and landing on John's shoulder. "That's not a problem, *cheri.*"

"Thank you," Lily murmured.

It was hard to believe a family was that accepting, but here they were right in front of her. The fear in her heart eased a bit, but not much. Ray still had not spoken to her since the night before. Her body remembered his hands, his mouth, his tongue and she shivered every time a memory surfaced.

As if she'd conjured him from her imagination, suddenly he was there, filling the room and her heart. He was dressed in brown from head to toe. Even his expression could probably be called brown.

"Where did you get off to, boy?" said John as he set his mug on the table and looked at Ray with narrowed blue eyes.

"I was helping Trevor with the tack."

"Sounds like an excuse to miss the birthday party to me." John humphed as he took a big gulp of coffee.

"Pa, you know I'm no good around kids, and—"

John cut him off with one swipe of his hand. "That's a load of shit and we both know it. Pardon me, Lily."

Lily nodded, too fascinated to pretend she wasn't watching the play between father and son. Francesca continued to wash dishes and hand them to Lily to dry.

"You love kids or you wouldn't have kept Melody. Now what's really the situation?"

Ray turned to leave the room with a scowl.

"Don't you dare walk out of this room, boy."

"I am thirty-six years old, Pa. I am not a boy."

"I don't care how old you are. I am looking for an explanation of what's going on here." John was the gentlest, kindest man she'd met, but now he looked like he could wrestle a bear and win. "I found you in the middle of the night in the kitchen with your hair all mussed, your shirt inside out and a bite on your neck. And somebody moved a barrel in the pantry a good six inches so it's up against the shelf. Miss Lily's a nervous wreck today and looking like she's lost her best friend. Now tell me what you're going to do about it."

Lily held her breath, waiting for Ray to tell everyone she was a loose woman. She even imagined herself on the train heading back to New York, crying and alone.

How could John do this to her?

"Pa, this isn't the way I wanted to do this."

"Get it done."

Ray put his hands on his hips and turned his scowl on Lily. She jumped, bumping into Francesca and nearly putting the older woman into the sink of warm water and soap.

"Will you marry me, Lily?"

Time simply stopped. Lily stared at Ray with her mouth hanging open. Did he just ask her to marry him?

Marry?

"I know I act like a horse's ass and that I'm as rough as the bark of a tree, but I figure we rub along good together. Melody sure likes you and so does my family."

Her voice seemed to have left her body. His eyes cleared for a moment and Lily saw into him. Into the *real* Ray. A scared, lonely man who had deep, ancient scars that may never heal. A man who needed a helpmate as much as a wife, someone who understood that when he gave, it was all he could give.

Someone like Lily.

"Say something, sunshine."

Lily cleared her throat. Her whole body was jumping inside like popcorn. He asked her to marry him. Was it enough? Could she live with a one-sided love?

Was there a choice?

"Yes, Ray, I believe I will."

Francesca whooped and threw her arms around Lily, hugging the stuffing out of her. John stood, smiling, and shook hands with Ray.

"It's for the best, boy. She's a good woman. Be a great mother and wife."

Ray nodded, still scowling. He walked over to where his mother was hugging Lily and hovered there until they parted.

"Can we talk alone?" he asked Lily.

She was afraid she knew what he was going to say, but nothing could keep her from going with him. She walked up the stairs ahead of him, her palms sweaty, her head spinning and her heart aching.

When they got to the room he shared with Brett and Trevor, he held the door open for her. She walked in and he followed, closing the door. Before she could even open her mouth to speak, he had her in his arms and was kissing her like a man possessed.

"I'm not going to share you with anyone," he whispered against her lips. "If you become my wife, then you're only my wife."

Lily was reeling from the kiss and completely confused by his words.

"What are you talking about?"

He grasped her arms and held her away from him. "I *won't* share you."

"Of course not. I wouldn't even dream of ever being untrue to my husband."

He stared into her eyes with his sharp gaze for a minute or an hour, she couldn't tell which. He seemed to be reading her soul, looking for a hint of a lie or whatever else he thought he might find. She hoped he didn't peer too deeply and see the scars her soul had carried for so long.

"Trevor was getting friendly down there."

"Trevor? He's a charming man, Ray, but that's all. The rest of me belongs to you."

It appeared to be what he wanted to hear, because before she knew it, they were on the bed and her skirt was up around her waist. His hand landed between her legs, in the slit of her drawers. With one swipe, she was instantly hot and wet for him, all he had to do was touch her and she was on fire.

"Ah, God, you're so ready for me…"

He unbuttoned her dress and his hot mouth suckled her breasts while he freed himself from his pants. With one thrust, he plunged in. A storm of sensations buffeted her from all sides. Sizzling, wet and wild. His lips and teeth scraped and laved her nipples while his hard cock slid in and out, faster and faster.

"Come on, Lily, come with me." His breath gusted past her ear then he bit her lobe.

Her nails scraped against his back as her body clenched and flexed around him. She felt the coil inside her grow tighter and tighter.

"Yes, mine. You're mine," Ray intoned.

The coil suddenly snapped and she was awash in pleasure, bucking against him. He shouted hoarsely as he reached his own peak, plunging deep. Waves of pleasure rippled through her body as Ray pulsed inside her. His body trembled against hers. Several minutes passed before she could even take a deep breath. Lord, she couldn't believe every time they joined, it was better. No, not better. More intense.

As the tremors subsided, her fingers uncurled from his shirt. She realized they were fully clothed, in the middle of the day, and just had sex in Ray's parents' house.

A wave of panic assailed her and she started pushing at him.

"Easy, Lily. It's okay," he said.

"No, it's not. I don't want your family to think badly of me. Please." She hated that she sounded so whiny.

He leaned up on his elbows and looked down at her, his expression unreadable.

"They wouldn't. They all love you."

She felt her heart pick up speed again. "All of your family?"

He knew what she was asking.

Do you love me?

He withdrew from her body and stood, helping her to her feet. She felt a bit empty inside. He walked over to the washstand and poured water in the basin. As she waited there with her heart on her sleeve, he handed her a wet washrag. After a quick wash, they straightened their clothes.

"Don't expect too much of me, Lily. My heart doesn't have a lot to give, but you'll never want for anything." He reached up and tucked a few stray hairs into her chignon at the back of her head.

"Rebecca did my hair this morning." She tried to keep her voice steady when her heart was aching.

"You look beautiful." He kissed her gently on the lips, then on the forehead. "I'm glad you said yes."

"There wasn't any other answer I could give."

ଓ ଛ

Ray was wrong. There was a member of his family who did *not* love her.

Melody.

"I don't want a mama."

Melody sat on a chair in the kitchen in her normal dirty trousers and shirt, black hair every which way, with a mutinous look on her face. Her lip was pooched out and her scowl could frighten birds. The battle had only begun.

"Regardless if you want a new mama or not, Lily is going to be yours," Ray said sternly.

"But, Pa. It's just you and me, we don't need her." She pointed one grubby finger at Lily who sat on the chair opposite the girl.

Lily was pale, and her whiskey eyes were filled with compassion, anxiety and a touch of doubt. Ray grimaced and turned his gaze back to Melody.

"I know you like Lily, Mel. Think how great it will be if she's your mama now."

Melody stood and stomped her foot. "You can't marry her."

Ray sighed and took Melody by the shoulders. "Yes, I can and I will. Tomorrow actually."

Melody appeared shocked and then absolutely devastated. She pushed at Ray so hard he fell on his ass.

"I hate you! I hate Lily!" She ran from the room and out the door into the snow without a coat or hat.

Ray looked up at Lily. "That went well."

Lily stood and held out her hand to him. With a mighty grunt, she helped him back on his feet. He dusted off his pants with his hands while a sigh worked its way up from his toes.

"I'll go find her," he said.

"No, you won't. I'm her problem, not you. Let me try."

Ray's first instinct was to say no. Melody was his daughter, but he needed to start trusting Lily. This was a first step.

"Take her hat and coat with you."

Lily saluted and snapped her heels together. "Yes, sir."

"Not funny."

She shrugged and smiled, then leaned up and kissed him quickly. "I love you, Ray."

Then she was out the door with Melody's coat and hat, and, dammit to hell, a big piece of Ray's heart in her hand.

CR ☙

Every time she walked outside, the cold slapped her in the face. Lily shivered inside her warm wool coat and marched determinedly toward the barn. She knew that's where Melody was. She had seen her out there before, playing in the barn with the cat, Patches. Although the sun was shining, there was not a scrap of warmth to be found outside. She thought it might take months for her to get used to the cold. Perhaps even years.

Lily took her time walking to the barn since she didn't want to fall in the snow again. Especially without Ray to rescue her, she thought with a grin. A few extra minutes also gave Melody time to calm down. Lily remembered very well how she felt at the age of nine after her mother remarried. That's when her life really became a living hell she didn't escape for two years.

Her boots squeaked on the snow as she finally made it to the barn door. Pulling it open, she peered inside the gloomy interior. She heard a few horses whicker, some shuffling of hooves and an occasional thump, but no child's voice and no cat's meow.

After entering the barn, she shut the door behind her and waited for her eyes to adjust. When she could see what was on the floor in front of her without falling, she walked forward, looking in each stall as she passed. Horses glanced at her with what she thought was horsey curiosity, but none bothered her, thank God.

Lily found Melody in the last stall beside a huge black horse. She sat in the straw with the calico cat on her lap, huddled and shivering. Although frightened to death of the horse, Lily unlatched the gate and swallowed her fear long enough to enter the stall. Keeping a wary eye on the animal, she tiptoed around him slowly until she reached the girl.

Lily sat on the hay and handed the coat and hat to Melody.

"Your father and I were worried about you in the cold without a coat."

Melody took the coat and hat, shoving them on with enough force to pop seams.

"I don't expect you to say thank you; however, I wanted to remind you that it was proper manners to do so. I'm going to tell you a story, Melody. A secret. This is going to be between you and me. No one else knows this secret."

She could tell she had the girl's attention. She stopped stroking the cat and simply stared at the wall of the stall.

"My father was a gambler. A really bad gambler actually. He made money occasionally, but not enough to support my mother and I. So we begged a lot and slept in many alleys and barns. He wasn't a bad man, just misguided and weak. He was shot and killed in a card game when I was nine. My mother was even weaker than my father. I used to be the one to get food and a place to sleep. Without my father, she fell apart."

Melody turned to look at her. "Your pa died when you were nine?"

Lily nodded. "Yes, and we couldn't afford a coffin, so he was buried in a pauper's grave somewhere in Mississippi." The thought still caused a sharp pain in her chest, like a small knife had been thrust in. She had loved her father dearly, even if he was never a good father.

"So then what happened?"

Lily put her arm around Melody, who snuggled in close to her. She felt the child shivering and was heartily glad she had some warmth to share with her.

"We were in Mississippi where the gambling is near the Gulf. My mother was like a lost puppy, whimpering and pitiful." A bad taste filled her mouth at the memory. "One night while I was out getting scraps from the restaurant in the hotel, my mother met a man named Archibald Darvey."

Even saying the name made her throat hitch as her gorge rose. Lily was convinced he was a spawn of Satan sent to Earth to punish every person he ever saw.

"Archibald was not only a bad man, he was an evil man. My mother fell under his spell—he was very charming at first. But his true colors came out a week after he married her." She swallowed hard.

"What happened?" Melody asked.

"Someday I might share more with you when you're older. But I told you that story to let you know that I have been you, Melody. I know exactly how you feel right now. Scared, uncertain and believing that I'm going to take your father away from you."

She cupped Melody's small cheek in her hand. "I love him, Melody. As much as I love you already. I know I'm not your real mother, but I hope we can try. Will you give me a chance?"

"Is it true you lived in an orphanage?" Melody blurted.

"Yes, sweetie, I did."

"Was it horrible?" Melody's dark eyes lit with curiosity.

"No, it wasn't horrible. The nuns were the kindest, gentlest people I had ever met. I was fortunate they took me in and taught me everything."

"So you're not a nun?"

Lily chuckled. "No, I'm not."

"Will you tell me about them? The nuns, I mean. I don't know any."

"Sure, but can we go inside the house? I think my fanny is frozen." Lily spoke the truth about that. The cold had seeped through her coat and dress.

Melody stood quickly, setting the cat down, then looked back at Lily with her head cocked.

"I guess we can give it a try."

Lily's heart felt lighter than it had all day. She smiled and held out her hand to Melody.

"Oh, help me up. I think I'm stuck."

Melody pulled and Lily pushed. That's when things went wrong. One of them, Lily wasn't sure which one, stepped on the cat's tail. The cat screeched and jumped on the horse's hind leg with its claws bared. The horse whinnied loudly and kicked to try to dislodge the cat.

It was as if time slowed down. Lily saw the horse's hoof heading straight for Melody's head. She moved faster than she ever thought possible to push the girl out of the way. The last thing she remembered was incredible pain in her hip and thigh, and the door of the stall rushing up to meet her. Then all was black.

☾ ☽

"Paaaaaaaaaa!"

Ray looked up from his coffee and immediately stood, knocking over the chair. He was halfway across the room before the back door burst open and Melody skidded in with snow-covered shoes.

"Pa! Help me, please! I can't move her and Uncle Tyler's horse is gonna kick her again. I tried to m-m-move her, but I couldn't. There's blood, Pa."

Ray didn't wait to hear the rest, he was out the door before she finished talking. His heart lodged somewhere near his throat and he almost forgot to breathe. He slammed into the barn, heading straight for Sable's stall. He heard the big horse whinnying like he was in pain, with a lot of grunts and thunks.

He saw Lily on the floor partially out of the stall, lying as still as a stone. Her bright blue hat forgotten in the dirty straw beside her.

Sweet Jesus!

He hadn't even stopped running before he grabbed her and pulled her out of the stall completely. Tyler and Jack were right behind him. Tyler jumped into the stall and took charge of his gelding. He heard the soothing murmur Tyler crooned to the horse, and Jack asking Ray if Lily was okay, but he didn't acknowledge anything but her.

Lily.

Ray knelt down next to her. She had a gash on her forehead and it looked as if her nose was really broken this time. Her face was as pale as milk, making the sprinkling of freckles stand out like dots of brown paint. He yanked a handkerchief out of his back pocket and held it against the bloody mess. She was breathing, but out cold.

"Melody!" he bellowed.

She appeared from behind Jack, looking absolutely terrified.

"What happened here, girl?"

"W-we were talkin' and then we stood up, and the cat got scared and scratched Uncle Tyler's horse. He was gonna kick me and M-miss Li-l-lian pushed me out of the w-w-way." Tears streamed down her reddened cheeks and she sobbed between words. "I th-think the horse kicked her and she fell on the stall d-d-door."

Jack picked her up in his arms and started rubbing her back. "It's okay, Mel. It's okay."

The horse kicked her somewhere. Probably in the back or legs. He had to get her inside so Nicky and his mother could take a look at her. Praying he wouldn't hurt her any worse than she was already hurt, Ray stood with Lily in his arms.

"I'm s-s-sorry, Pa," Melody said.

Ray didn't answer her. He was already out of the barn and heading toward the house, his precious bundle clutched in his arms.

He burst into the house, careful not to let the doorjamb hit Lily.

"Mama! Nicky! I need you!"

Ray took her upstairs to her bed, laying her down gently. He was removing her shoes when his mother and Nicky came in at a run.

"What happened?" Nicky asked.

"Sable kicked her and she slammed into the damn stall door. I think her nose is broken and she's pretty banged up."

They pushed him out of the way and started stripping her.

"Get out, Ray," said Nicky.

"Don't talk to me like that, Nicky," he bellowed. "She's going to be my wife. I have every right to be here."

"You're in the way, so move," Nicky ordered.

"I'm not going anywhere," Ray shot back.

Francesca scowled at them with blazing green eyes. "If you're going to fight, both of you get out. This girl needs help and the two of you are not helping."

Duly chastised, Ray tried to swallow the fear that had invaded his throat. Lily was so still, lying there on the bed. When his mother pulled up her dress, and tugged down her knickers, he sucked in a pained breath. Her hip and thigh were already purpling with an enormous bruise. A horseshoe of angry welts were at the center of the bruise.

"We need to pack some snow on this to keep the swelling down," said Francesca. "Ray, go get a bucketful."

Ray wanted to stay in the room, but knew his mother was right. They needed to keep the swelling down. He opened the door and ran into his brothers, Tyler, his father and the children in the hallway.

For some reason that escaped logic, they all started talking at once. He couldn't even think through the cacophony. The noise was deafening.

"Enough! Mama and Nicky are looking at her. She got kicked by a horse and hurt her head on the stall door. Now get out of my way so I can go get some snow for the swelling."

The door opened behind him. Nicky poked her head out and frowned at everyone. "Jack, go get some towels. Trevor, go get Mama's sewing kit."

She closed the door and the silence lasted for a moment, then everyone started talking again.

"If you want to help Lily, go away. Jack and Trevor, get what Nicky asked for," Ray shouted. He pushed his way through everyone, intent on getting a breath of fresh air and the snow for his future wife.

My woman.

Not even married yet and already worried about losing her. It was hard. Too hard. He didn't know if he could do it again.

CHAPTER ELEVEN

Lily could not remember where she was. All she knew was her rear end and her face throbbed in tune with each other. The pain in her behind was excruciating. It felt like Archie had taken a cane to her again. Mama must be out looking for business.

"Mama? Archie?" she asked.

"Shhh, it's okay. Relax," came a soft, feminine voice.

Lily just couldn't focus. She was lying on a soft bed, somewhere, so she knew she wasn't home. The sheets and the bed were too soft.

"Who the hell is Archie?" an annoyed man responded.

"Ray, if you can't be nice, leave the room," another man replied.

"Make me."

Someone sighed. "Will you two stop it? I am sick of hearing it," said the woman.

"Sorry, Rebecca," the annoyed man grunted.

"Sorry, Becky." The other man sounded much more sincere.

"You'd think you two were five instead of grown men."

There was silence for a minute. Lily tried to concentrate on the voices. The annoyed man sounded so familiar. The memory was like a dandelion puff in the wind though and she just couldn't run fast enough to catch it.

"Why don't you two go check on your children? Lily is obviously still talking in her sleep. If she wakes up, I'll let you know," the familiar man said.

"I think he's trying to get rid of us."

"And with good reason, Jack. You're being a pest," the woman, Rebecca, teased.

"You wound me, Angel," replied Jack.

Lily heard a kiss then a chair scrape. A gentle hand touched her cheek.

"She'll be all right, Ray. You heard what your mother said. Her body just needs to heal itself."

Lily wanted to cry from the gentleness in that voice, that touch. It had been so long since she'd felt such softness. Her closed eyes pricked with tears and she struggled to control them. Her head pounded and her nose ached something fierce. Crying would make everything worse.

A door closed and all was silent. Lily opened one eye and saw a man sitting on a chair next to her. He was big, with wavy reddish-brown hair, at least a day or two's growth of whiskers on a strong jaw, and the most intense green eyes she ever remembered seeing.

They flicked to her and she was startled to see concern, regret and something else in the depths of those eyes.

"You're awake," he said. "You had us all worried there, sunshine."

"Did Archie cane me again?"

Now he looked startled. "Nobody hit you. A horse kicked you in the…er…hind end and you slammed into a stall door and hit your face."

Relief coursed through her. Now if only she could remember where she was, and more importantly, who this man was. Sleep started creeping over her like a warm blanket and she struggled against it.

"Where am I?" she mumbled.

"You're in a bed in my mother's house. We came here for the twins' birthday, remember? You and Hope were sharing. She's been bunking down with the younger girls though downstairs so they don't disturb you."

Lily wanted to ask who he was, but the blackness swallowed her in a roar and she surrendered to sleep.

CR ഔ

Lily slept. This time it wasn't that deep unconsciousness that had plagued her since yesterday. Now she was simply sleeping. A wave of relief washed through him. Mama had been right—Lily just needed to heal herself.

"I know who Archie is."

Ray almost jumped off the chair in surprise. Melody had crept up to stand next to him and he never heard a sound. Damn, that girl was like a ghost.

"You snuck up on me."

She shrugged. "Aunt Bonita taught me how."

He nodded. Bonita was half Lakota Sioux and liked to teach the children some of her Indian ways. Ray thought it was a good thing for the children to learn whatever they could from her.

"Who is Archie, Mel?"

She scooted onto his lap and laid her head on his shoulder. He anchored his arm around her tiny waist. He inhaled her childish scent of oatmeal, soap and milk.

My daughter.

No matter what anyone ever said about Melody, she was *his* daughter.

"He's a bad man. Miss Lillian told me he married her mama and that he was evil."

An evil, bad man who married her mother and obviously took a cane to her more than once. Lily surely knew what pain was. No wonder she thought she'd been caned when she woke. She likely knocked her head around enough to mix it up.

"I think he hurt her."

Ray sighed. "I think he must have hurt her too, but we won't let that happen again. Will you help me protect her?"

"Yes, Papa, I will. I don't want Miss Lillian to be hurt again either."

Melody snuggled in deeper against his chest. It had been so long since she had wanted to be held or cuddled. He simply accepted it as a change, perhaps brought about by one tiny, voluptuous woman who he intended to marry.

"Do you love her, Pa?"

Well, shit. He should have expected that. How to explain to his five-year-old daughter what love and trust meant.

"I like her, Mel. We can make a good life together."

She harrumphed against his collarbone. "Grandma would call that no answer at all."

He chuckled. "When did you get to be forty-five instead of five?"

"I'm only five, Pa. If I was forty-five, I'd be almost dead already."

Ray held back the chuckle this time, because it would have turned into an all-out laugh.

"Will you let her be your new mama?"

She didn't answer.

"Will you *try* to let her be your new mama?"

A baby soft sigh gusted past the skin on his throat.

"I'll try, Pa, but it ain't gonna be easy."

Melody was like a wise old woman in the body of a child. She surprised the hell out of him all the time. He squeezed her tightly for a moment.

"Ouch! What're you doing, Pa? Trying to squish me?"

"Sorry, Mel, just thinking what a lucky father I am."

"Oh, yuck, you're going to be mushy now? I'm leaving."

Melody scrambled off his lap and darted out of the room. He watched her go with a shake of his head. Then he turned his gaze back to his future wife. Some wedding day this turned out to be.

CR ED

Lily awoke to bright sunshine. Her left eye felt sore and tight. She reached a hand up and felt a bandage, underneath that she could feel the outline of stitches. She opened her eyes, blinking until she could focus on the chair in front of her. Next to the bed, sleeping in the chair with his head back, mouth open and snoring softly, was Ray. It was probably the last thing she expected to see by her bedside. He looked strangely at peace, although distinctly uncomfortable.

Lily tried to focus on how she ended up in the bed, obviously hurt, with Ray as her nurse. She had been in the barn with Melody and that big black horse and a screeching cat, then pain. She remembered dreaming of Archie and Mama. It had been fifteen years since she'd seen them, but they danced like demons at the edge of her memory. She tried to roll over, but the pain in her hip and thigh stabbed at her like a thousand knives. Lily groaned and shifted her weight.

The pain was familiar. It was as if she'd been caned. That's why she'd been dreaming of Archie. The humiliation, the thwack sound of his cane on her bare legs and behind. The refusal to make a sound while he did it. She clenched her fists on the bed and forced herself to remember how strong she could be.

"You need help?"

She was embarrassed to have Ray find her in her nightgown, half out of the covers, groaning and moaning. It could be worse. She could be naked too.

"Yes, please," she finally admitted. "I feel like a babe learning to roll over."

He chuckled and gently helped her turn on her side.

"Who's Archie?"

The question dropped to her stomach like a lead ball. Her tongue felt as dry as cotton and her throat closed up.

"Oh, shit, I didn't mean to blurt that out, sunshine. I…well, the thing is you were talking in your sleep or whatever it was. Mel said he was a bad man who hurt you. Jesus, I'm starting to sound like Nicky. Frigging magpie."

Lily decided right then and there that she might as well tell him all of it. If they were going to be married, she wanted to begin with no secrets. There was too much ugliness in her past to hide it any longer. Once she started, the words just tumbled out.

"My father was a gambler, a pretty poor one. He was killed in a poker game when I was nine. My mother remarried within months. Archie was my stepfather. He...uh, he used to beat my mother and me. He got her hooked on opium and made her sell her body to anyone willing to pay a few bucks for her. I hid from him as much as possible, but when I was eleven, I um...matured early. Since Archie wanted to have me under him, he figured other men did too."

Ray stared at her, growing paler and paler as she spoke.

"Are you telling me that your stepfather turned you into a whore?"

"For one night he did. I don't even remember the man, other than he had pale white skin, was flabby and smelled of onions. I ran away and lived on the streets for a week. When I returned, I found out that my mother had killed Archie and then took enough opium to kill a horse. That's when I was sent to St. Catherine's. Do you want me to continue?"

His eyes were shuttered. "Is there more?"

"Yes." The painful lump in her throat grew larger by the minute.

"Finish it then." His voice was hard and curt.

"I tried to fit in at St. Catherine's, but I was an ignorant, foul-mouthed daughter of an opium addict and whore and a dead gambler who had his head blown off in front of me. I started getting into fights constantly and was always in the infirmary. That's where I met Sister Margaret. She had infinite patience for me and always had time to listen to whatever came out of my mouth. When she,"—Lily swallowed. Hard.—"died, I decided right then and there to be a teacher. She opened the world up for me, Ray, of books and people and places I will never see, but know because of books."

"How did she die?"

She was hoping he wasn't going to bring that up, but in for a penny, in for a pound. *Just finish it.*

"We were ice skating in the park and I fell down by the thin ice. She tried to pull me to safety, and I panicked. The ice cracked under her weight and she fell in. She drowned saving me."

It was so quiet, Lily could hear her heartbeat thumping like a locomotive.

"So your mother was an opium-addicted whore, your father was a gambler, and your stepfather sold you as a whore when you were eleven. Your mother murdered your stepfather then committed suicide. You lived in an orphanage where you accidentally killed your favorite nun and teacher."

Saying it out loud was more painful than she imagined. What an ugly life she'd had.

"Anything else?"

Lily closed her eyes tightly for a moment, then opened them. "All my other governess positions were terminated because of my clumsiness or the fact that the father couldn't keep his eyes off my breasts long enough to pay attention to his wife."

Ray stared at her with his fathomless eyes. He stood and walked to the window, rubbing his neck with both hands. He likely had a crick in it from sleeping in that uncomfortable chair.

"I know I'm not a prize catch for a wife, Ray. Things went awfully fast for us. I want to let you know that you can step out of this marriage. I would understand completely and not be angry about it."

She would have a broken heart to go with her broken noggin and rear end, but at least the parts would all match. She almost laughed aloud at her absurd, maniacal humor.

He turned and looked at her. "Do you still want to marry me?"

"Yes."

There was no hesitation on her part. The answer would always be yes.

He nodded. "Then rest up for another few days and we'll get married."

Beth Williamson

Ray walked out of the room without another word, without a kiss or a hug, or even a handshake. Lily felt like she had just been interviewed by a desperate man looking to fill a hole in his life who was willing to settle for whatever dredges came through the door.

Ray took a drag from the cigar and blew the smoke out into the frigid night air. He'd been hiding from the family most of the day. Since Lily revealed a past so shocking, he had to flee or break down in front of her.

What was it about the Malloy children and their choice of spouse? They seemed to pick the most troubled, scarred, crazy or unusual people for a husband or wife. He was apparently no exception. Why couldn't one of them pick a normal, everyday Jane who was sweet, demure and dreamed of nothing but serving her husband?

Nope, he had to go pick a twenty-six year old with a past that would make someone's hair curl right after they finished gasping at the horror of it.

The thing that really confused him was after all the ugliness, she still shone like a new penny. Bright, upbeat and willing to live her life to the fullest.

She was like sunshine and he was like a thundercloud. His father pressured Ray into offering for her, but after he'd done it, it felt…like the right thing to do. Even now, after he found out about her past, it felt right.

He just hoped his darkness didn't overshadow her light.

CR SO

The wedding took place on a Wednesday morning just after breakfast. Lily walked with a limp and had more than a few stitches in her forehead, but she stood straight and tall, well as tall as she could, next to her bridegroom. It was going to be her only wedding so she wanted to be at her best.

In two days, Rebecca had whipped together the most beautiful dress Lily had ever seen. She felt like a fairy princess in blue silk with dark gray piping. She even made her a matching petticoat with blue ribbons on it.

Ray had done his best to be distant. He had even gone home for a few days before the wedding to take care of business. Melody stayed behind and became Lily's helper. She helped fetch water, helped her stand and walk, and even helped her empty chamber pots. The child was amazing.

Ray's family was incredibly supportive. They nursed her, chatted with her and made her feel like a part of their family although they'd only known her a week.

Nicky and Tyler's son, Noah, arrived the evening before. He was a tall young man with light brown hair and brown eyes, not particularly outgoing like the rest of the men. He mumbled a polite hello and she hadn't seen him since.

A minister named Robert Campbell came to perform the ceremony. He was apparently a good friend of Ray's parents. He had silvery hair with bright brown eyes. They stood in the living room before the ceremony getting acquainted when he asked Lillian what her full name was. That was when the reality hit her. She was going to have her name on a *marriage certificate*. She was going to be married.

Her stomach clenched and her sparse breakfast of biscuit and tea threatened to reappear. The minister must have seen something in her face because he ushered her off to a corner of the living room and plopped her down in a chair.

Within moments, he was back with a glass of water. After a few sips, she felt better. He patted her shoulder until she looked up at him.

"Are you ready to get married, Lillian?"

She pushed the unnecessary fear away and thought about how much she loved Ray. "Yes, Reverend, I am."

He smiled and nodded. "I'm glad to hear it. Raymond hasn't had an easy time of it since he married and divorced, but I think you will turn that around for him."

"Thank you."

He walked away and Lily gazed into her glass of water. The ripples from her shaking hand echoed in the glass. The ripples from today would echo through her life.

A shadow fell over her.

"You about ready, Lily?"

Ray looked uncomfortable in his black suit and yanked at the collar with one calloused finger. She couldn't read his eyes. They reflected nothing but the sunshine coming in from the window behind him.

"Yes, I'm ready, Ray."

They were married within twenty minutes. When Reverend Campbell said, "You may kiss the bride," way down deep inside her something flared to life. The thought of Ray's lips on hers, of his body touching hers, lit a fire that began to burn brightly.

He cocked his head and regarded her with those hard eyes, then cupped her face and kissed the stuffing out of her. His lips were relentless, plundering, rubbing, pulling her closer and closer to losing control. Her nipples peaked as her body's arousal grew. Her nether lips grew moist and she ached for his touch, for his skin against hers.

A cough and a snicker from behind them shocked like a pinch in her behind. She jerked in surprise and her eyes flew open. His pupils were dilated with arousal and his nostrils wide as he breathed in sharply. His thumb ran back and forth across her swollen lips.

"We'll finish this later." With one last, hard kiss, he stepped back and allowed the horde to descend on her.

After all the congratulations were over, the minister asked them to sign the marriage certificate. As the heavy gold band weighed down her finger, she signed her new name.

Mrs. Lillian Malloy.

She glanced up at Ray, his usual serious and annoyed self, and then at Melody. She looked ready to tear off the matching blue dress Rebecca had made for her. Her beautiful black hair was combed and in pigtails tied with blue ribbons. However, she wore her boots, which made Lily smile.

Ray's hand at the small of her back felt exactly right. As the hugs and kisses rained around them and on them, Lily realized that she finally had what she'd always wanted.

A family.

∝ ∞

A small reception followed for family and friends. Not many were invited, but every person accepted. Lily felt less overwhelmed than the day before since she'd met most everyone. Still, there were so many people, she felt a little stifled and escaped outside for a breath of fresh air.

The sunshine sparkled off the white snow, temporarily blinding her as she stepped onto the porch. A hand grabbed her elbow.

"Steady there, Miss Lillian." Noah's voice came from her right. "You nearly fell down the steps there."

Lily's cheeks heated. "Not too unusual for me, Noah. I'm, ah, a bit clumsy."

She turned to look at him and was surprised again by how gentle Noah appeared. Most of the Malloy and Calhoun men were aggressive and loud, except for Brett who was surprisingly quiet but intense. Noah was different.

"It's pretty cold to be out here in only a dress." Noah draped his coat across her shoulders and his body's warmth immediately chased away the chill she hadn't realized she had. Lily saw the man Noah was growing into. His broad shoulders topped a wide chest and narrow waist. He still had some filling out to do, but the muscles were building already.

"Thank you, Noah. You're very kind."

He shrugged. "My ma and Nicky taught me manners. I try to use 'em as much as I can."

There was an awkward silence when Lily tried to think of something to talk about, but Noah saved her.

"I know I ain't supposed to—I mean I'm not supposed to say anything, but I need to tell you something," he began.

Curiosity got the better of her, and Lily gave him her undivided attention. "Of course, anything."

He smiled and the thought struck Lily that he was a handsome boy— man actually. Noah was soft-spoken, polite and mannerly, some lucky woman was going to find a legacy when she found Noah.

"I wanted to say thank you for marrying Uncle Ray." He held up a hand when she started to speak. "Hang on. In the five years I've known him, I have *never* seen him crack a smile, laugh, or even just look like he was having fun. I think I about fell out of my chair when I saw him grin at you yesterday."

Lily wasn't surprised. "You've never seen him smile?"

Noah shook his head. "Other than Melody, life just wasn't giving Uncle Ray what he needed I guess. I didn't know that woman he was married to, but whatever it was she did made him a hard man. Too hard."

Noah took her hands into his larger ones and looked her in the eye. "I just wanted to say thanks. I think he really needed you."

A feeling of rightness coupled with peace and joy spread through her. She'd been nervous, downright scared and uncertain. Just talking with this young man made it clear her decision was the right one.

CR SO

They went home a few hours later. Ray gruffly told her he didn't want to spend his wedding night sharing a bed with his little brother. Although she was still sore and dreaded riding in the wagon, Lily was glad to go home.

Home.

She was astonished she had an actual home to go to. A real house with a husband and a new daughter. A house had finally become a home.

Francesca hugged her tightly and whispered in Lily's ear. "Love him for who he is. Be patient. And don't be afraid to kick him in the fanny if he acts like a jackass."

Lily bit her lip to keep from laughing. Everyone kissed and hugged her like she was truly a daughter, sister, aunt and friend. Noah winked at her and grinned widely at Ray's scowl.

With a twinkle in his eye, Trevor kissed her on the lips. She heard Ray growling behind her, but he needn't be worried. There was no fire, no heart-pounding excitement from kissing Trevor. It was like…well, like kissing her brother.

Ray gently lifted her into the wagon and settled her and Melody in. Lily sat in back on piles of blankets and a pillow given to her by her new mother-in-law. As they waved goodbye, Lily swallowed back a few tears.

Her entire life had changed over the last week and a half, and it was all part and parcel with becoming a Malloy. Trevor rode along with them to help out for a few days and give the newlyweds some time together. Ray kept darting sharp glances at his younger brother, who just smiled and waved.

Lily's initial enthusiasm about going home began to wane rather quickly. The two hour ride seemed to last two days. By the time they reached the Double R, Lily was ready to get out and walk the last half mile. She felt like the horse had kicked her all over again. She was sore, tired and ready for a hot bath.

The first inkling that something was wrong was the seats on the front porch. They were turned around backwards as if someone didn't want to watch the sunset. Ray frowned when he stopped the wagon and hopped down to get Lily and Melody out of the back.

"The chairs…"

"I know. I see them. Stay here while I take a look around." He glared at Trevor. "Go check the barn."

Trevor saluted and hopped off the horse, heading for the barn with his hand resting on the pistol strapped to his thigh.

Lily was grateful to be standing instead of sitting. She stamped her feet on the snow, willing the circulation back to her legs. Ray went around to the back of the house.

"I'm cold, Miss Lillian."

Melody's little face was white with cold and her lips were an unnatural shade of blue. Lily didn't see Ray anywhere, so she made the decision. The child needed to be warmed up. Truth be told, so did she.

"We'll go get a fire started."

She took Melody's hand and together they made their way into the house. When the door swung open, Lily was surprised to find it already warm inside. A fire crackled merrily in the living-room fireplace. She could also smell coffee somewhere, old coffee that had been sitting long enough to get sludgy and rancid.

"Somebody's in our house," whispered Melody.

Cold fingers of fear tickled Lily's spine. Her stomach squeezed up tighter than a walnut and her hands got very, very damp.

"Who the hell are you?"

The harshly worded question nearly knocked her off her feet. After trying to catch her heart and stuff it back in her chest, Lily turned and saw a blonde woman with an elaborate chignon standing in the doorway to the kitchen.

She was beautiful with big blue eyes, a perfect bow-shaped mouth, slender yet curvy, with a smirk that looked well used. Her burgundy dress was of the highest quality, a fact Lily knew immediately. All of her previous positions were with people who could afford fancy, expensive dresses. This woman's face was familiar in some way. Lily searched her memory.

It hit her with the force of the kick from that black horse. She was familiar because Lily had met her sister.

It was Regina. Ray's ex-wife had come home.

CHAPTER TWELVE

Ray found a few unfamiliar footprints in the snow, but otherwise, the house looked secure. He knew Rafe and Clyde were likely out riding the fence this time of day. It meant somebody else was in the house. His internal warning bells were clanging like crazy. Something was definitely *wrong*.

When he stepped back around the front of the house, he found Lily and Melody gone. *Son of a bitch!*

Married three hours and she was already not listening to him. He saw their footprints leading into the house and followed in a hurry. God forbid anything happened to them.

He burst through the front door and slammed it right into the hole he had made weeks ago when he found Trevor and Brett there. Only this time it wasn't Trevor and Brett.

His stomach knotted up and his entire body jerked with a kick to his heart.

Regina.

She sat in the chair by the fireplace like a queen on her throne. She was as beautiful and perfect as ever. Her blue eyes were as cold as the wind blowing behind him and the look on her face was enough to send him screaming from the house. It was a punch that stole his breath and his ability to speak.

"Raymond," she trilled. "About time you got in here. I was just speaking to this woman." She inclined her head toward the sofa. Lily sat there, pale as milk with her hands clutched together in her lap. She stared into the fire, away from him.

Sweet Jesus.

"I think there was a child here too, but she ran off." Regina flapped her hand in the direction of the hallway.

He heard the clock ticking somewhere as he stared at his ex-wife. The woman who destroyed his life, his future. The acid churned in his stomach as his shock turned to anger.

"That woman is my wife and that child is my daughter. What the hell are you doing here?" he growled.

She smiled and it looked more like a sneer. "Your manners have not improved, Raymond."

"Neither have yours. Get out of my house."

"Was that *our* daughter?" she asked.

"None of your fucking business. Get out of my house."

"Aren't you going to let me see her? She is *my* daughter, isn't she? Are you going to keep me from her?"

Lily stood and walked out of the room. Ray longed to follow her, but he needed to take care of the cougar in his living room.

The cold from the open door caressed his neck. He shivered and finally closed the door. Taking a deep breath, he turned back to Regina.

"Are you deaf? Get out of my house."

She rose and sashayed toward him like a predator stalking its prey. That awful smile was still on her face. As she got closer, Ray wound tighter and tighter. By the time she stopped in front of him, he was afraid he was going to strike her. His fists clenched so tight, his knuckles popped.

Up close, her face had a grayish tint to it and he saw lines around her eyes and mouth that hadn't been there five years ago. She was perspiring around her hairline. Regina didn't look good. In fact, she looked like she was sick.

"What's wrong with you?"

"Concerned about my welfare, Raymond? How kind of you. I had a touch of the flu, but I'm better now," she said. Running her finger along his shoulder, she smirked again. "Especially now that you're here."

Ray forced himself to stay still when all he wanted to do was push her away and out the door on her perfect ass.

"What do you want, Reggie?"

Her smirk twitched. Direct hit.

"Don't call me that, Raymond. You know I don't like it."

"The door is behind me. Just turn the knob and walk out."

He turned to step away from her. He *had* to. She grabbed his arm and he couldn't stop his reaction. He wrenched away and took two steps back.

"Don't ever touch me!"

She held up her hands in mock surrender. "My, my, you didn't used to say that to me, Raymond." She grinned and leaned in to whisper at him. "In fact, you could barely keep your hands off me."

"Me and a few dozen others," he snapped.

Her mouth tightened. "That's not very nice."

"Neither was finding out that your wife fucked anything in pants. Or that your daughter was the seed of one of those faceless men who you took between your thighs."

Oh, God, it hurt. It hurt more than he thought it would to see her again. Regina looked over his shoulder and smirked.

"You shouldn't listen at doors, dear daughter."

"Pa?"

Melody's voice scraped across his skin like a rusty saw, full of pain and confusion. He swung around and saw her standing in the hallway, the dress traded for a pair of overalls and a sweater. Her dark, dark eyes riveted on him.

"You're not my pa?"

"Yes, I am."

"Oh, don't listen to him, Melody. You are not his daughter."

"Shut up, you bitch!"

Melody looked between them and started crying in great, gulping sobs. Lily appeared behind her and scooped her up in her arms. She glared at Ray and Regina.

"You should be ashamed of yourselves. She is a person too, not just a thing to wound each other with."

They disappeared into the hallway and a door closed softly, but he still heard the sound of Melody's wrenching sobs. Ray's were locked inside him howling to escape.

"Get out of my house. Now!"

"You would kick me out when it's getting dark outside? You didn't used to be such a hard man, Ray."

He counted to ten and then counted to ten again. "I don't care if it's midnight, I want you out of here. I'll go hitch up your horse to your buggy. Get your shit together. You have five minutes."

His entire body felt like a raw, gaping wound again. Ray turned and went back outside into the cold. As he walked toward the barn, he wiped the tears off his face. He would not waste any more on Regina.

CR SO

Lily sat on Melody's bed, rocking and soothing the hysterical child. Her mouth was as dry as cotton; she was shaking and sick to her stomach. Her wedding day had turned into a nightmare.

She had been so happy and now the day sat like ashes in her mouth. Why did that woman have to come? Why did she have to be such an awful, vicious person?

Melody's sobs turned into sniffles and she was finally quiet. Lily realized she had fallen asleep, her little face wet and reddened from her tears. Lily had to fight back her own. She laid Melody down and tucked a quilt around her, then kissed her sweaty forehead.

"Sweet, sweet Melody," she whispered.

Lily didn't want to go back out there and face that woman, but she was Ray's wife now and had to stand beside him, for better or for worse.

She squared her shoulders and went back into the living room with her heart pounding and her cowardice scratching at her back.

Regina sat on the chair, watching the front door. One wisp of blonde hair landed on her cheek. Her perfection was marred by the twisted snarl on her face. She turned her sharp blue eyes on Lily. A shiver made its way up from her toes at the coldness in that gaze.

"So you married him, hm? Pity you."

"No, you've got that backwards. *I* pity *you*. You had him, and you threw him away."

Regina laughed roughly. "You pity me? I'm not the one wearing a poorly made rag, married to an ox of a man, with a bastard daughter in the middle of nowhere. And who's been using you as a punching bag, sweetheart? I probably know the answer to that one already."

Lily walked a little further in the room, pressing her trembling hands into her dress.

"I am wearing a handmade gift made by a wonderful lady, married to a good man with a beautiful daughter, in a house that is as sturdy and strong as its owner."

"You're blind."

Lily shrugged. "You see only the ugliness in the world. I see the beauty."

"You certainly are a ray of sunshine, aren't you?" she sneered.

Lily couldn't help but smile at that. She was Ray's sunshine.

"I like to think so."

"And apparently consider it a compliment."

The door swung open abruptly and Lily nearly jumped out of her shoes. Ray appeared in the doorway like an avenging angel. Trevor was behind him with an expression she'd never seen him wear. One of anger and malice, directed solely at the former Regina Malloy.

"Your carriage is outside. Get out. Now," Ray snarled.

Regina stood and opened her mouth to say something, but instead her eyes rolled back in her head and she collapsed to the floor.

"That's not gonna work, Reggie. Get up."

Lily ran to Regina's side and checked her over.

"She's unconscious, Ray. Her pulse is fluttery, she's clammy and her skin tone isn't good."

"Well, shit. Some wedding night this is gonna be."

The door slammed behind him and a puff of frigid air gusted past her. Lily gazed down at the woman who had shaped Ray's life. How could one person have so much power?

"Trevor, please help me move her."

"I don't really want to touch her, Lily."

Lily looked up sharply at her new brother-in-law. "I don't give a damn. Pick her up and bring her to the guest room. We are still Christians and will give charity where and when it's needed."

Trevor stared down at Regina with a scowl. "What's wrong with her?"

"I don't know, but leaving her on the cold floor is certainly not going to get her better any faster, now is it?" Lily snapped.

With a thunderous scowl that reminded her of Ray, Trevor picked her up and walked toward the bedrooms.

"She's light as a bird. I can actually feel her bones. Maybe she's not eaten in a while."

Lily knew what was wrong with Regina, but wasn't ready to share the information yet. Trevor laid her on the bed and stepped back. Lily shooed him out of the way.

"Go check on Melody, then see if Ray needs help."

Trevor cocked one eyebrow at her. "When did you get so bossy?"

Lily sighed. "Please."

"Give a yell if she wakes up and starts clawing you."

Lily shook her head to dispel that particular image, then went to work. Unbuttoning Regina's dress a bit, Lily took a cold cloth and wiped Regina's face and neck. After ten minutes of Lily's ministrations, Regina started to come around.

"Billy?" she mumbled.

"No," Lily replied. She sat on the edge of the bed and watched while Regina slowly regained consciousness.

"Where am I?"

"You're in the guest room on the Double R Ranch."

She shifted her gaze to Lily. In the depths of those cold blue eyes, Lily saw a frightening monster that lived inside. She forced herself to sit still when all she wanted to do was run. She *knew* that monster. Had lived with that monster. Hated that monster.

"How long have you been using opium?" she asked.

Regina looked startled, but recovered quickly. Her mask of cold indifference slipped over her face.

"What makes you think I use opium?"

Lily shrugged. "I'm not sure if you drink it or smoke it, but you are definitely a slave to it."

Regina's gaze raked her up and down. "What would a little church mouse like you know about opium?"

Her temper tried to break free, but Lily held it back. "I know a lot about opium. More than I ever wanted to know. I will feed you, allow you to stay here until the morning, but after that, you will leave this ranch forever." Lily stood, shaking with rage. "You've caused enough pain in this family to last a lifetime and I won't allow you to crawl back here and cause more."

Lily left the room with her head held high, proud that she hadn't slapped and screamed at Regina.

CR SO

Ray was currying his horse when Trevor came into the stall. For the first time in a long time, there wasn't a smile on his face.

"What are you going to do?"

Ray sighed. "Damned if I know."

"Drive her into town and dump her at the doc's. He'll take care of her."

Ray shook his head. "Lily probably won't let me. She's too nice."

Trevor sat on an overturned bucket. "That she is, and you'd better make damn sure you keep her. There aren't many like that running free, big brother."

A surge of jealousy tasted bitter in his mouth. "You wanted her?"

Trevor rolled his eyes and picked up a piece of straw, spinning it between his thumb and forefinger. "Oh, for God's sake, Ray. She's beautiful, smart and the best cook in Wyoming next to Mama."

"She's mine."

Trevor chuckled roughly. "Don't I know it. For some unknown reason, she's in love with you. I reckon I'll never understand that."

Ray didn't respond. Lily had told him she loved him, but he still kept part of himself locked away from her. And now this auspicious beginning to his marriage. Jesus please us, it couldn't get any worse.

"Lily made me put her in the guest room."

Well, he was dead wrong. It just got worse.

"Son of a bitch! Why the hell did she do that?"

Trevor shrugged. "I didn't want to, but for a little woman she sure can bark out orders when she wants to. I expect that bitch will be there until she's well enough to travel."

"Not a chance."

Ray tossed the curry brush at his brother and stormed out of the stall. It was time he and his bride had a chat. He took long ground-eating strides toward the house, the snow squeaking beneath his boots. He walked into the house ready to bodily throw Regina out into the snow if necessary.

He found Lily standing in the kitchen staring out the window into the orange and pink rays of the sunset.

"Before you say a word, I've told her she's leaving in the morning. What she has is only going to get worse, but I can't in good conscience send her out in the cold night air especially after her fainting spell."

That took the wind right out of his sails. He let out a breath and walked up behind her. A whiff of lavender tickled his nose as the scent of Lily washed over him. His body immediately tightened like a bowstring.

The baby soft hairs on the nape of her neck waved in the wind of his hot breath. His cock woke up and began slamming against his trousers, hungry for his woman. Hungry for Lily. The heat from her body mixed with his and the temperature rose steadily as his passion ignited.

He bent down and kissed the back of her neck softly. She started slightly, but then leaned into him, inviting him.

My woman.

Goose bumps danced down her skin as he trailed kisses along her neck to her ear, where he nibbled and licked until he heard a soft moan from her throat. The sound went straight to his groin. His hands slid from her shoulders to her waist and he pulled her flush against him. She hissed with pleasure and rocked slightly. The cleft of her perfect ass nestled him like she was made to be there.

As he switched sides and began kissing the left side of her neck, her head lolled back against him. His hands, eager to join in, crept up to her breasts. The beautiful, bountiful breasts that were now his. Every day and every night. Wishing it was his mouth, he tweaked the rising nipples between his fingers, rolling them back and forth. Her arousal scented the air, pulling him deeper into the passion around them.

"I need you, Lily."

"Yessss."

She turned in his arms and wound her arms around his neck. Her lips sought his blindly and his body screamed in response. Their mouths met hard and hot. Tongues tangled and bodies rubbed.

Without another word, he scooped her up in his arms and strode from the kitchen. Their lips never lost contact as he navigated down the hallway to her bedroom...*their* bedroom.

He was completely out of control. His body had taken over and his mind was boiling in a pot of sexual heat so hot he felt scorched.

Ray kicked the door shut behind him and made a beeline for the bed. He laid her down gently, mindful of her bruises, and started working on the buttons on the dress. The damn things were too small for his big fingers, so he fumbled and grew frustrated. God, he needed to feel skin. When he grabbed the lapel, she tsked against his lips. "Don't you dare rip this dress. Rebecca made it for me."

"Help me, then. I don't have the patience for it," he growled.

Within moments she nimbly unbuttoned it, then looked up at him with her eyes darkened with passion.

"I love you, Ray."

He slid her dress down her body, slowly peeling her clothing away layer by layer until she was deliciously nude. The pale skin contrasted with his dark hands as the calluses contrasted with the softness they touched. Her pale pink nipples were tight and begging for attention. The shadows in the room spread around her, as if waiting for his exploring hands and mouth to find her. He lay between her legs and ran his hands across her moist skin.

Ray kissed her belly while his hands took possession of her breasts. As he kissed his way along the downy skin, he nipped and licked, tasting and teasing her arousal. Small goose bumps broke out across her legs the closer he got to her pussy.

"Ray, I'm not sure..."

He didn't respond. Her scent and his own excitement was enough to make him as hard as steel. The need to taste her, to touch her, to bring her pleasure pulsed through him. He kissed all around the purple bruises on her thigh and hip, sorry she had to endure such pain.

When he finally reached her heated core, he spread the lips with his thumbs. Beautiful, pink and glistening with arousal, he ran his thumb lightly across her sensitive nub. She shivered and a small kittenish mewl erupted from her throat.

Ray ran his tongue around her clit, then suckled it hard, and she nearly took his head off with her leg.

"Easy, Lily."

She made some kind of strangling sound of agreement and he went back to work.

He alternately laved, suckled and nibbled her while his thumb slid in and out. Lily tasted of heat, sex and woman. Her legs trembled while her body grew hotter with each stroke. As she neared her peak, he switched his thumb for two fingers.

Sweet God, but she was tight. *So tight.*

Ray suckled and licked her until she came like a glorious rainstorm, bucking and twisting against him. Her juices flowed as her hands clenched on the bedcovers. She moaned his name and shuddered over and over.

His own arousal was hard enough to split wood. He needed her. *Now.* With a haste he hadn't known since his youth, he tore off his clothes and was back on the bed with her in a blur of motion.

Lily was so warm and soft, he just about melted right into her. Instead, he drove his hard cock into her moist heat, then paused, buried to the core, and rested his forehead on hers. Embarrassed by his haste, even now holding back his orgasm by sheer force of will. His blood flowed like a river of fire, pushing him to move, to thrust, to fuck.

"I'm sorry."

She ran her hands along his back, squeezing his ass lightly.

"Nothing to be sorry about. Only if you plan on stopping. Please, Ray, love me."

It was all he needed to hear. With a shiver of pleasure that snaked up his spine, he began to move within her. Sliding in and out, nearly completely, before plunging back in. Each time he entered her, she closed around him and a bolt of pleasure thundered through him.

Lily drew her knees up and opened herself wider. He returned the favor by going deeper.

My woman.

She tightened around him like a fist, driving him to the edge of insanity. He knew she was close, but he couldn't hold back much longer.

"Lily, I'm so close, tell me…"

A keening cry of pleasure echoed around them as she clenched over and over, sending him plummeting into the abyss of an orgasm so intense, he stopped breathing. Time slowed down. Every pulse, every throb, every shudder ricocheted through him a thousandfold.

When he was finally able to take a breath, the rush of blood to his head was enough to make him dizzy all over again. He rolled off her and pulled her against his body, snagging the quilt from the bottom of the bed to cover them up.

Within moments, he fell asleep with his new wife wrapped in his arms.

CHAPTER THIRTEEN

The light scratching on the window roused Regina from a slumber. Need clawed at her belly and she desperately tried to will it away. She rolled to the edge of the bed and sat up. After the urge to vomit passed, she stood and walked to the window.

She opened it and peered out into the moonlit night.

"Billy?"

She could barely see, but it looked like him. A few inches taller than her, Billy was built like a bull, with a face to match. But he was smart and clever—two things that drew her to him like a moth to a flame.

"Yeah, baby, it's me. Did you find the cash?"

The frigid night air woke her in a hurry. Her hunger became a screaming beast that needed to be fed.

"Not yet. Do you still have some left? In the pipe?"

"Only a little. It ain't enough though. In a week, it's gone, do ya hear me? We need that money."

Billy was her companion and lover. Well, for a year at least, maybe. Time tended to blur a bit when you were an opium eater. Regina had found herself wrapped in the sticky tendrils of the drug after she broke her arm shortly after arriving in San Francisco. Within six months, she was moving from laudanum to the opium dens in Chinatown. There were a lot of things she had done for the beast living inside her.

One of them was being a companion to Billy. He was a hard, dangerous man who did whatever he needed to, whenever he needed to. This crazy idea was his. Get her ex-husband's stash of cash he kept from the sale of horses to the Army. When she'd left, it had been enough to keep them in opium for almost a year. Since Ray didn't believe in banks, it was probably ten times that now. Billy wheedled her into coming back although he knew she swore she'd never step foot in Wyoming again.

"What time is it?"

"I don't fucking know what time it is," he whispered harshly. "Just find the goddamn money and get your lazy ass out of there. I'm tired of talking with those small town idiots."

Regina rubbed her temples with her hands. "Don't yell, Billy. You'll wake up those fools out in the bunkhouse."

He grabbed her wrists in a painful grip and yanked her forward. She stared into his dark eyes, feeling the anger and hate coming off him in waves. For a moment, she thought he was going to reach up and snap her neck. Instead, he kissed her hard, enough to draw blood. She moaned against him as her body combated another hunger.

"Give me some, Billy. Please," she begged against his mouth. "I can taste it on you. You had some already. It's been nearly a day for me."

He shoved her back until she fell on her behind on the hard wooden floor.

"You're not getting any until you get that money, bitch."

"Fine," she mumbled, climbing back to her feet. "Raymond is a creature of habit. He kept his money in a jar in the pantry. I was about to go look there when they showed up."

"That's my girl," he crooned. "Now who's the lovely little girl in the room next to you? She'd fetch a mighty fine price from Mr. Shen."

Regina felt a twinge of concern but it passed quickly. Her priorities had to be straight, and getting that money was first on the list. Besides, Billy was right. She would fetch a good price since Mr. Shen liked his girls very young.

"She's my daughter."

Billy's eyebrows shot up nearly to his hairline. "I didn't know you were a mother."

"I'm not."

His smile glinted in the moonlight. "Excellent. You get the cash and meet me out here in ten minutes. I'll make sure sleeping beauty is out and take her for a ride with us. You can be a pretend mommy for a week."

Regina shuddered at the thought. "Fine, but you will share with me what you've got. I need some, Billy. I...I'm starting to see things that aren't there and I fainted earlier."

"You'll get what you deserve, after you get the cash, got that, Queenie?"

Another nickname she loathed, but she accepted it from Billy. After all, she was a queen. It was time to seize control of the peasant's funds like any good monarch.

"Ten minutes," he warned.

"Ten minutes."

Regina hunted for her shoes on the floor until she found them, then slipped out the bedroom door as quietly as possible. The house was as silent as a tomb. She slid down the hallway toward the kitchen, set her shoes on the table and went into the pantry. Raymond always kept a candle and matches in there. She quickly found them, reaffirming her notion that he was, and would always be, a creature of habit.

After lighting the candle with shaking hands, she pressed hard into her yowling stomach with one fist. She held the flame up until she saw the old silver tin on the top shelf then stood on her toes so she could grab it. Setting the candle down on the shelf, she pried the top open and peered inside. The roll of bills made her body rush with anticipated pleasure.

There was so much. A lot more than she expected. Raymond had obviously done quite well for himself, although she couldn't tell that from his wife's wardrobe. Regina took the money out, then carefully replaced the tin. Splitting it in half, she folded the bills in her right hand and shoved it down in her corset. The other half she put in the pocket of her dress.

Regina carefully put everything back in its place then headed for the front door. The silence in the house was only broken by the ticking of a clock and her pounding heart. She was so close to getting away with what she came for. Close enough that she salivated at the prospects of all she could get with the money tucked by her breasts. With a smile, she helped herself to the heavy coat hanging by the door. Regina deserved a coat that nice, something a queen would wear.

Cracking the door, she peered out and heard nothing. She headed into the blackness of the night toward the barn, cursing inwardly at the unrelenting cold of Wyoming. When she got to the barn, she stepped inside and waited until her eyes adjusted to the dimness. The smell of hay and horse shit made her stomach roil.

"Billy?" she whispered.

She heard a thunk and a grunt from the darkness.

"Some bastard was out here, tried to stop me from taking the horse we rightfully stole."

Regina walked toward his voice and nearly tripped over something on the ground in front of her. She belatedly realized it was a body.

"Did you kill him?"

"No, but he won't be moving for a while. Did you get it?"

Regina reached into her pocket and held the money out toward him.

"Yes, and it's a small fortune."

The money was snatched out of her hands.

"Get in the damn buggy. We've got to get out of here and on that first train out of town before your lover wakes up."

She grimaced. "He hasn't been my lover since before we were married."

Billy laughed, the oily sound sliding around her. "Let's go, Queenie."

"Smoke?" she asked, hating the whining tone in her voice.

"No, but I've got something else. You'll get it as soon as we're on our way," he promised.

Within minutes, they were in the carriage, riding through the cold. Life was already better now that she knew Wyoming would be a bad memory by the end of the day. Tears from the bitterness of the air snuck out of her eyes. She ignored them after Billy handed her the small vial. She opened it with shaking hands. In one gulp, she emptied the contents. As the thick liquid made its way down her throat to her stomach, Regina finally began to relax.

She ignored everything but the euphoria rushing through her. She even ignored the small bundle with dark hair in the back of the carriage.

CR SO

Lily woke with sunshine on her face and a heavy, warm arm across her waist. She smiled sleepily and turned to look at her new husband. He was awake and studying her with his bottomless eyes.

"Good morning." She felt suddenly shy.

When Ray blessed her with one of his rare smiles, her whole heart gave a tremendous thump. She had completely fallen in love with this man even though he was hard, stubborn and impossible to read at times.

Best of all, he was truly her husband now. She had a home and a family.

"It's late. The sun is pretty high in the sky," she said.

"Yup, that it is. Melody is probably already off in the barn with Trevor since it's quiet in the house." He waggled his eyebrows. "Think of anything we can have for breakfast?"

Lily felt her cheeks redden even as her body softened at the naughty suggestion. Although they had sated themselves twice during the night, she was willing and able to make love again.

"I think I can." Taking a deep breath, she pushed herself up and threw one leg across his. The surprise on his face almost made her chuckle.

"You know more than I think you do. I keep forgetting that."

She smiled. "I've never been able or wanted to use that knowledge before. Until now."

As Lily leaned down and brushed her already hard nipples against his chest, the door to the bedroom burst open. Lily screeched and dove under the sheet. Ray cursed and tried to cover them with the quilt.

"Trevor, what the hell are you doing?" Ray paused. "Jesus Christ, what happened to you?"

Lily peeked out in time to see Ray jump out of bed, stark naked. She tore her gaze away from his finely crafted behind to look at Trevor. One side of his head and face were covered in blood. Her stomach fell to her feet as dread jumped into bed with her.

"I don't know. Some sidewinder was in the barn last night and bashed me upside the head with something. I think it was a shovel. Regina's carriage and horse are gone."

Ray frowned. "Was it her that hit you?"

"I don't think so. It was too big to be her—had to be a man." Trevor tried to shake his head and ended up weaving on his feet and clutching it instead. "Damn, that hurts."

Lily, unmindful of her modesty, dashed from the bed and threw on some clothes as quickly as she could. She turned, buttoning her dress, to the surprised eyes of her husband and Trevor, who had a small grin on his face.

"There's no time for this. We've got to check on Regina and Melody. Was anyone in the barn this morning or outside?"

"Just Clyde. Nobody else around. Rafe spent the night in town."

Ray looked like Lily had hit him. "Check on Melody?"

He took off running toward Melody's bedroom. Lily went to the room Regina had slept in. She knocked before opening the door. She was unsurprised to find the bed and the room empty.

A bellow of sheer rage and pain rocked the house. Lily turned and ran in the direction of the sound.

Oh dear God, please.

When she entered Melody's room, she found Ray on his knees, clutching Melody's pillow. To her dismay, the room was empty, the blanket and quilt missing. Trevor stood next to him with stricken eyes, pleading with her to do something.

Lily knelt down with her hip screaming at her—which she ignored—and placed her hand on his big shoulder. He was shaking, but his muscles were rock hard.

"Ray…"

"That fucking bitch took my daughter," he said against the pillow.

"We'll find her. We need to look for signs in and around the house. We'll go into town and find out if they've been there."

A sob burst from him, muffled by the pillow.

"That fucking bitch took my daughter," he repeated a little more hoarsely.

Lily lightly rubbed his shoulder. It was like caressing granite.

"I know, but we'll find her. Together. We need to start looking now."

She felt the absolute urgent need to find Melody, a clawing ache inside her. She loved that girl as if she were her own. The raven-haired pixie's loss would nearly destroy her. She hated to think what it would do to Ray.

If he lost his daughter, she knew whatever chance they had for a good marriage was lost as well. His world revolved around his daughter, without her, his world would collapse.

He finally lifted his face and looked at her. The naked agony in his eyes hit her like a ton of bricks. Her own pain was nothing compared to his and she started crying for him. He was dry-eyed, apparently unable to shed tears, although she was sure he was crying on the inside. He reached out and caught a tear with his finger.

"What do you mean together?"

Lily was surprised. "I mean together. You and I. *We will find her.*"

She saw the war in those pain-filled eyes. He wanted to accept her comfort and support, but it was a big chasm to cross. Lily leaned forward and kissed his forehead.

"I love you, Ray. We will not give up until we find her."

He nodded then pressed his face into the pillow again. "It smells like her. Dammit, Lily, I...I can't lose her."

"You won't. We'll find her, I promise. Now let's get a bandage for Trevor, then we will search every nook and cranny to make sure she's not here."

He took a deep breath and let it out on a shudder.

Lily felt her heart kick when he nodded.

"We will find her." She believed every word she spoke.

ငၢ ၵာ

Lily was unsurprised to find that Regina had stolen her beautiful navy wool coat the sisters had given her. She ended up wearing an old coat of Ray's that hung down nearly to her knees. Ray discovered his money tin in the pantry had been completely emptied. He was fortunate she didn't know about the second tin, or Regina would have taken two years worth of savings.

Rafe showed up and Clyde came in. The five of them searched for an hour. As suspected, Melody was nowhere to be found on the ranch. Trevor found footprints in the snow by Melody's window and the bedroom Regina was sleeping in. It confirmed that the same man was in both rooms.

There were carriage tracks from the barn leading toward town. The theory was that the man was in cahoots with Regina and they had taken Melody for unknown reasons. Ray was controlling his rage, although it was a constant battle.

Lily saw him clench his teeth hard enough his jaw kept popping. He kept his head and watched everything with his keen eyes.

"We need to head to town. You stay here," Ray said as he headed for the barn with Trevor, Clyde and Rafe.

Lily's anger rose and danced on her tongue. "You will *not* leave me here to wait, Raymond Malloy. I am coming with you whether you like it or not.

She is my daughter now too and I love her. Besides that I have experience with people like Regina."

Ray's head snapped around and he looked at her with narrowed eyes. "What do you mean, 'people like Regina'?"

"She's an opium eater, Ray. She had the same symptoms as my mother did."

Ray's mouth dropped open as did everyone else's.

"Opium? That Chinese stuff?"

"It was brought here originally from China, but it's become a horrible, awful drug that makes you change into a monster that only craves more of it."

Ray stalked back toward her. "Did you think you needed to tell me this earlier?"

"I forgot. We were looking so hard to find Melody that it slipped my mind."

"Slipped your mind? This is my fucking daughter we're talking about. Not a quilting bee!" he shouted.

"Don't you yell at me. This is for better or for worse. I will not be shouted at like a dog during the worse."

She ended by thumping her fist on his great chest. He snatched her up and slammed her against him, his lips on hers, hot and scorching. She wound her arms around his neck and hung on for dear life. Her body cleaved to his like she was a part of him. In the frigid morning air, he was a haven. He was home. He was hers.

He pulled back and looked into her eyes. "It ain't gonna be easy."

"I'm pretty tough, Ray."

"So I noticed."

She smiled tentatively at him and he gave her one last kiss then set her back on her feet.

"Be ready to leave in fifteen minutes," he ordered.

Lily scurried into the house to pack. She had no idea how long it would take to find Melody, so she packed several changes of clothes and food for them.

The Malloys were on the hunt for their missing cub.

CHAPTER FOURTEEN

When the Double R crew made it into Cheshire, everyone went off in different directions, intent on a purpose. Lily was assigned the task of checking at the general store, since Regina was the owner's daughter she may have gone there.

Ray looked at her with his shuttered eyes and Lily glimpsed a portion of the pain he was going through every minute that passed.

"We'll find her," she repeated, then kissed him quickly and went to Goodson's store.

It seemed like a lifetime ago that she had been there with Melody. The day the boys had called them names. The day Lily's life had changed. So much was different now. She strode purposefully to the counter to speak to the older woman who had waited on her previously.

"Excuse me," she said.

The woman looked up and Lily could now clearly see the resemblance to Regina and her sister. They all had similar coloring and eyes. However, this woman's face held a wealth of sadness and anger.

"What do you want?" Mrs. Goodson snapped.

"I'm sorry to bother you, but there is an emergency and I need your help."

The other woman regarded her skeptically. "What emergency?"

"Melody Malloy was kidnapped during the night last night. We are searching around town to ask if anyone has seen her."

Mrs. Goodson snorted. "That little half-breed? Not likely."

Lily's temper began to bubble again. "As far as I know, that little half-breed is your granddaughter. I should think you would be concerned that she was missing."

Mrs. Goodson actually appeared shocked. "What are you talking about? She's not my granddaughter. She's the get of some Indian squaw and that excuse for a man, Raymond Malloy. Ruined my daughter right good, he did."

Lily squared her shoulders. "That little girl is Regina's child, the 'get' of your daughter and an Indian man. Her father is Raymond Malloy—a better man you will never meet. He raised her as his own and now she's missing. Regina was here yesterday and apparently involved and we were hoping you might have seen her."

Now Mrs. Goodson looked as if she'd been slapped. "You're lying. That's not Regina's child. She would never abandon her own child. Her child died at birth. And she wasn't here in town. What are you talking about?"

"She was at the Double R yesterday. I myself spoke with her and helped her. This morning Melody is missing and so is Regina. We think there was a man involved as well."

"Why are you spouting such lies? Who are you?" Mrs. Goodson shrieked.

"I am Lillian Malloy, Ray's wife. I am also Melody's new mother. I would appreciate any information you might have."

Mrs. Goodson came around the corner and started pushing her out of the store. "You get your fancy manners and your lies out of my store. Regina was not here yesterday. She lives in Paris. And that bastard half-breed is not her child."

The door slammed in Lily's face. The glass nearly hit her in the nose. Well that didn't work out like she planned. She hadn't lost her temper though. The only good news was that Mrs. Goodson hadn't seen Regina—no one was that good of an actress.

Lily's next stop was the restaurant. She wrapped the too big overcoat around her tightly and trudged through the snow toward Hannah's

Restaurant. Her hip was bothering her, but she ignored it. Her own personal discomfort was nothing compared to what Melody might be going through.

That particular thought allowed a sob to jump from her throat. She swallowed it back down and concentrated on finding information, not permitting her heart to run wild.

CR Ω

Ray left the stable in an even fouler mood then he'd gone in. The only thing Will Bentley could tell him was that a couple had rented the carriage two days ago and returned it sometime last night. It was here in the morning. The folks who rented it had not paid for the two days they'd had it and Will complained loud and long about that.

"Hey, Ray, hold on!" Will called.

Ray turned around and waited impatiently. "What?"

Will walked toward him with his uneasy bowlegged gait. With his frizzy gray hair, mud-brown eyes and nervous tics, he was not a man with many friends. However, he'd always been kind to the Malloys, a favor they returned.

"There was a blanket in the back."

Ray's heart began to pound again. "What blanket?"

"It was a light blue color, wool. I put it in the basket inside."

Ray went tearing back into the stable, nearly tripping over the doorway in his haste. He grabbed the handle of the basket under the bench and yanked. Melody's blue wool blanket tumbled out into his arms. Her scent surrounded him and he had the overpowering urge to weep.

They had been here, and they had Melody. He snatched the blanket and threw the basket.

"Where did they go from here?" he demanded.

Will scratched his head. "I dunno. I weren't here when they left the buggy. I told you that already."

Ray bit back his angry retort. "Were there footprints? Something that told you which direction they went?"

"Oh, yeah, I guess they did. There were a fresh coat of snow this morning. The tracks went toward the station."

The train.

Yes, they would have wanted to get out of town as quickly as possible.

"Thanks, Will."

Ray started running toward the store, realizing halfway there that he was running to Lily.

He found her exiting the restaurant. She looked so tiny in his old jacket, her silly blue hat shining like a beacon on her head. It was one of the things he loved about her. That silly hat.

He loved her?

When the hell had that happened? He stopped dead in his tracks, completely poleaxed by the thought. It was the hardest, most excruciating time of his life, and suddenly his heart decided to start working again?

Lily spotted him and hurried over. Her brows furrowed and she worried her lip between her teeth.

"I haven't found any information yet, Ray. They weren't in the store or the restaurant."

"They returned the carriage and the horse sometime before dawn. Will found Melody's blanket in the back and said their footprints headed to the train station," Ray blurted. "We found a clue."

He scooped her into his arms because he couldn't do anything else. He hugged her tight against him, stuck his nose in the crook of her neck and breathed her in deeply.

"That's wonderful," she squeaked. "What are you doing?"

He kissed her hard and set her back down.

"Let's go to the station and talk to Melvin."

Together they headed toward the station, elated by the crumb of information they had. If they were lucky, Regina and Melody were still there. Ray tried not to let it in, but hope crept its way across and nestled in his heart.

The station was small, and only had two trains a day. One going east and one going west. The eastbound train came in the afternoon. The westbound train came in the mornings. As they walked up the steps, Ray remembered that this was where he'd met her. Lily.

My woman.

The feelings, fears and uncertainties echoed around him. He would never have guessed that the next time they were at the depot, they would be husband and wife. He squeezed her small hand in his and led her to the door.

He opened it and they went inside, the heat from the small potbellied stove took off the biting edge of the cold. His stomach clenched when he realized there were no passengers waiting.

Melvin Cassidy had taken over the train depot ten years earlier. A forty-something strange, bespectacled man who kept to himself, Melvin had no close friends in town. However, he was very observant and never missed a detail. Ray was counting on him for information on his ex-wife and the missing piece of his heart.

Sitting on the stool next to the stove, Melvin glanced up from the book he was reading. Dressed in his standard white button-up shirt, vest and brown pants, he pushed the round glasses up on his nose and sniffed.

"Good morning, Ray," he said, then nodded at Lily. "Ma'am."

Lily nodded back at him.

"Melvin, this is my wife, Lily."

"I'm pleased to meet you," she said.

"I had a feeling I might see you, Ray." Melvin stood and laid the book down on the stool. "Had some passengers this morning."

Lily's hand tightened on his almost to the point of pain.

Melvin took his watch out of his vest pocket, looked at it briefly before snapping the case shut, then put it back in its place.

"Round about dawn, Regina came in. I was a might surprised to see her here, but she asked for three tickets to San Francisco."

Ray's stomach plummeted to his feet. The blood pounded through his veins furiously. He had to struggle to stay focused.

San Francisco? How the hell am I going to find her?

"There's something else, isn't there?" asked Lily from beside him.

Melvin nodded. "Yes, ma'am, there is. Regina was acting rushed so I asked her what was waiting for her in San Francisco."

"What did she say?" Lily calmly put her arm around Ray's waist. That's when he realized he was weaving on his feet.

"Paradise by the water. Don't rightly know what that means, but that's what she said."

Lily led him to the bench next to the window and urged him to sit. The world tilted and he was grateful to be able to sit his ass in a solid spot.

"Did you see anyone else?" Lily continued.

"When the train arrived, there was a man holding a child who came out of the shadows and stepped on board with her."

"Did you see what he looked like?" Lily was relentless, getting information they would need. Thank God he asked her to come to Wyoming. Thank God she said yes to being his wife. Without her here, he'd tear the place apart and end up in jail.

Melvin thought for a moment, looking at the ceiling with his brows furrowed. "Medium height, but very large man. Built like a bull if you know what I mean. Was wearing fancy duds too and a bowler hat. He had dark hair. I couldn't see much else because it was still sort of dark."

Lily smiled. "Thank you, Melvin. I cannot tell you how grateful we are."

"I had a feeling someone was going to come looking for Regina. She showed up out of the blue and hid in the shadows until the train came. What's going on?"

Lily squeezed Ray's shoulder. "Regina and her male companion kidnapped Melody in the middle of the night."

The color drained from Melvin's already pale face. "Little Melody? That's who that man was carrying?"

Lily nodded. "We're not sure why, but at least now we know where they're going. We'll need two tickets for the next train to San Francisco."

Melvin gulped and went behind the counter. "Absolutely."

"How much?" Ray reached into his pocket.

Melvin waved his hand in the air in dismissal. "No charge. This one's on me. I let them get on that train knowing something was wrong."

"But you couldn't have known they kidnapped Melody," Lily said.

"I could have contacted Jim at the sheriff's office."

Ray shook his head. "They would have stopped you. Believe me, they knocked Trevor upside the head with a piece of lumber. He needed a dozen stitches to close it up."

Melvin began to visibly tremble. "Lord have mercy, who did Regina fall in with?"

"The devil and his minions apparently," answered Lily.

After Melvin gave them their tickets for the following morning, Lily led Ray back outside. The snap of the frigid air cleared his head somewhat, but he still felt sick as hell. God, how were they going to find a five-year-old girl in a city the size of San Francisco?

"You need to eat something. Both of us do. Let's go down to the restaurant."

He blindly followed her, the only thought running through his mind was of finding Melody. The hopelessness sapped his strength, pulling him down until he thought he'd fall off the world.

"We'll find her."

Lily stopped and took his face between her hands. Her bright blue mittens were warm against his face. He stared into her eyes and saw love, determination and sheer stubbornness.

"Understand me, husband? We *will* find her."

He nodded, trying desperately to swallow the lump of pity that appeared in his throat. He grabbed her and hugged her tightly. Her arms wrapped around him as far as they could go and she squeezed.

"I hate to interrupt you two love birds," came Trevor's voice from behind him. "But we have found a whole lot of nothing."

He reluctantly let Lily go with one hard kiss on her cold lips.

"I believe you," he whispered.

Turning to his brother and friends, he started filling them in on the information they'd gotten from Will and Melvin. They all headed for the restaurant to warm up and fill up. The Malloys needed to prepare for what would happen once they reached San Francisco.

CR SO

Billy and Regina traveled to San Francisco in style thanks to Raymond's money. The kid started squawking the minute she woke up on the train so Billy fed her a constant bit of the precious stash to keep her sleeping and out of their hair.

Regina was in high spirits when they pulled into the train station. Billy carried the girl off and right into his waiting carriage without a single question from anyone as to what was wrong with her, which suited them just fine. When they got to their apartment near the Barbary Coast, Regina asked Mrs. Ping who lived downstairs to keep an eye on the girl. Her dark eyes were disapproving, but she agreed to do it. For a price of course.

Regina gleefully went to her favorite opium den, behind Shen's restaurant. She paid her way in. No one greeted her or asked where she'd been, but she immediately felt at home. Plopping down onto the pillows, she joined the party of three smoking from a rather large hookah in the Blue Room.

Within minutes, she was floating on clouds, watching as the dark-haired man beside her fucked the woman passed out on the pillow next to him.

Any thoughts outside the room fled as she enjoyed the smoke and the show.

CHAPTER FIFTEEN

They were nearly there. Lily recognized Oakland and knew that the bay was just ahead. She sat across from Ray in their compartment. Both of them looked like they'd been wrung dry and hung up to wrinkle. The last three days had been hard with no privacy, no respite from worry, and worst of all, the imagination of a parent knowing their child was in danger.

Ray had a haunted gloom to his eyes, dark bags grew deeper and deeper beneath them. New lines appeared on his face, making him appear haggard and drawn. She doubted she fared any better than he did.

"We're going to arrive in about half an hour," Lily said.

"You sound like you know what you're talking about."

"I do. I was here a long time ago."

"I didn't know you'd been to San Francisco before." Ray raised an eyebrow.

"Oh, there aren't many cities I haven't been to with my father's gambling."

"And?" he asked, obviously sensing there was a lot more to the story.

She shrugged. "He took me with him. A lot. That's how I know how to play cards. He'd use me…as a distraction of sorts. Even though I was little, I was entertaining. I'd sing for them too."

He grunted. "You have a nice voice. Distracts the hell out of me."

She smiled thinly. "Really? I'll have to remember that."

Ray stared out the window of the train. "Do you think she's all right?"

Lily's heart clenched painfully. "I hope she is. Melody is a strong, smart little girl."

"I want to kill them."

Lily reached out and patted his stiff knee. "I know you do. I'm having a hard time controlling that impulse too. What we need to focus on is getting her back, no matter what we have to do."

Ray nodded and ran his hands down his face. "No matter what we have to do. That doesn't sound good."

Lily knew they would probably have to do a lot of things she didn't want to do, but experience from her childhood told her they'd be necessary.

"It's not, but we're going to do it anyway."

"We'll find her," Ray said the words like a prayer.

"Yes, we will find her. And we'll get her back."

ൠ ൠ

After they arrived at the train station, Ray and Lily spent some time finding a map of the city and talking to the San Francisco Police. All they promised to do was keep an eye out for her. Ray appeared ready to do murder by the time they left the police station. Lily was just as frustrated.

Following another four hours of looking for information at City Hall for any establishment named "Paradise", Lily gave into the urge to rest since they were both swaying on their feet. Her mind and her wits were not at their best, and neither were Ray's. They needed sleep badly. It was getting dark and they didn't have a shred of information. She had to nearly drag Ray to a hotel in a not-so-nice part of town. Lily convinced Ray it was necessary because of the need to be near the Barbary Coast and Chinatown. She was sure they'd find Lily there since the evils of humankind lurked within their streets. He grimaced, but acquiesced to her request.

The Grand Hotel was not so grand, and it was pretty cheap. A dilapidated sign at the front heralded high quality rooms and beds. Lily knew

that was an untruth, but it was what they needed. The front desk clerk looked like an escaped convict and she swore the woman they met going up the stairs was a prostitute.

High quality indeed.

When Ray and Lily got into the hotel room, they discovered a small bed with dingy sheets that certainly hadn't seen a good washing in a while, a smell that would scare a dog, a scarred table and chair and a small washstand with a cracked pitcher.

"I hate this place," Ray grumbled.

Lily stopped him and stepped into his arms. "So do I."

"Why are we here again?" he asked grumpily.

"This is where we'll find her. Everything and anything goes on within the confines of this area. Believe me, I know." She knew all too well. Just being there gave her a bad taste in her mouth.

"Do you know your way around?"

Lily took a deep breath. "Yes, I think so. I know all the main streets and most of the side streets."

"Good. Don't leave my side, understand?" It sounded like an order, but said in a soft tone that Lily understood. Ray was out of his element and out of control.

"I know we'll find her, but Ray…I'm still scared."

Silence followed her statement. She wondered if he even heard her, then he spoke. "I'm scared, too." Ray's whispered admission echoed loudly through Lily's heart and soul.

His hands started moving up and down her back. The warmth and pressure relieved some of the tension. She sighed and snuggled closer into the crook of his neck.

"What's the plan, General?"

She smiled into his shoulder. "We're going to get some sleep. It's been two days since I saw you close your eyes. We need to be at our best to find her and we can't do it if we're tripping over our eyelids. Tomorrow we can go to the Barbary Coast and get some information."

He grunted. "I don't like waiting and I sure as hell don't like you being in danger."

"I can take care of myself, Ray. I lived in places like this for nearly half my life."

"I still don't like it, but I'll allow it…for now."

"You're bossy."

"So are you."

"I guess we're a good team."

Sounds from the street and the hotel echoed through the small room. Fear had sunk its talons into Lily, but knowing Ray supported her helped a great deal. Their connection had grown deeper, richer. The love flowed through them.

As she lay on the bed, she watched Ray undress. Aside from looking like a Greek statue come to life, Ray was peppered with small scars here and there. He ran his hands through his hair and stared through the window.

"We will find her. I promise."

His sad eyes looked down at her until her optimism apparently touched him. He sat on the edge of the bed, kissed her forehead and hugged her close.

"I hope you know what you're doing."

"Do you trust me?"

Ray leaned back and scowled. "That's a hard question for me to answer. I don't trust many folks, most especially women. I…" Ray paused and took a deep breath. "I…trust you, Lily."

The hesitancy of his response hurt a bit, but Lily took his words and held them close to her heart. She was sure Ray hadn't ever planned on trusting a woman again.

He hugged her once more, then let go and climbed over to the other side of the bed. He wrinkled his nose and looked at her with a raised eyebrow.

"Sleep on your clothes."

Ray nodded and snagged his shirt and pants, then lay them down on top of the pillows. Within moments, he was asleep. Lily lay awake for hours, praying they would find Melody in time.

CR SO

The day dawned quiet and gray, typical for San Francisco. The sun hadn't fought its way through the morning fog yet so the room was draped in shadows. Lily lay there for a few minutes, then the urgency of finding Melody hit her. She needed to find information without her towering husband glowering behind her, scaring folks. Before she changed her mind, she rose quietly and dressed in one of her newer dresses and left the room, trying not to make any noise. Ray said he trusted her, so he'd just have to understand that some things she needed to do alone. She sauntered downstairs, her street smarts coming back like an old friend.

When she reached the front desk, she had transformed into Lil. Her top five buttons were undone and her hair hung in waves down her back.

"Hey, handsome," she purred at the desk clerk. "I met this friend who said I could find paradise by the water. Ever hear of it?"

The young man's beady eyes widened as he eyed her cleavage hungrily.

"Paradise by the water? Nah, I don't know it."

Lily made a small moue with her mouth. "Oh, that's too bad. I really wanted to find it."

"I'll take you to a happy place. Let's go in the back."

She shook her head. "My man's asleep now but he can smell it when another man's been on me. Maybe tomorrow when he goes out?"

He shook his head jerkily, greasy hair flopping back and forth on his grimy forehead.

"I want a bath," Lily said.

"There's a bathing room on each floor, end of the hall. Water's probably not ready for the morning baths though."

"Hmmm… Can I go into the kitchen and check?"

He ran his hand along the bulge in his trousers. "Sure thing, doll. Want some company?"

"Tomorrow," she said as she winked and sashayed through the door to the kitchen. She felt his eyes on her behind and fought the urge to run. Instead she turned around and waved at him with her fingers. His hand fastened on his cock, pumping up and down slowly as she sauntered away.

Suppressing a shudder, Lily walked into the kitchen and winced as something crunched under her foot. Likely one of those big awful cockroaches. A young Chinese girl stood by the stove with four large pots on it.

"Hello there," she said.

The girl nodded, her dark eyes wary.

"I was hoping you could help me. I have a friend who says that paradise by the water is a place to go to be happy. Do you know it?"

The girl's eyes widened slightly and she stepped back, bumping into the stove. She yelped at the contact and stared at Lily with fear in her eyes.

"You no want to go there. Mr. Shen is bad man. Blue Room for bad people."

Blue Room? That must be the name of the opium den known as paradise by the water.

Trying not to smile at her success, Lily kept her face blank. "I know what it is. I need to find it though."

The young girl shook her head vigorously.

"You won't tell me where it is?"

The girl shook her head again. It was time to give a bit more information.

"I'm looking for a girl, five years old, who arrived yesterday on the train."

"What girl?"

"My daughter," said Lily, in her heart knowing it was true. "She was taken and I believe is going to be sold or auctioned. The woman who took her I believe was going to this Blue Room."

"Then you no find her," the girl responded.

"Please, help me. All I need to know is where it is." Her voice began to crack.

"I know nothing."

Lily decided to try another tactic. "I'll pay you. My husband has money, enough to pay you for what you make here for a year."

"He has one hundred dollar?"

Lily tried not to gasp at the amount. Using quick calculations, she realized how much a hundred dollars was to a Chinese immigrant. This child was making thirty-five cents a *day*.

"Two hundred if you tell me how to find the Blue Room and Mr. Shen. You can walk out of here with the money and not come back."

She was thinking about it, Lily could tell.

"Please, she's only five," Lily pleaded.

"You go get money."

Lily nodded and scurried out of the kitchen, back up to the room. Trying not to make a sound, she took Ray's wallet from his jacket pocket as it dangled from the side of the bed. Extracting two hundred dollars, she returned it to its place and ran back downstairs.

When she got to the kitchen, the girl was gone. Lily felt a sob jump up her throat and she clenched her hands around the money.

So close.

"Psst," came a voice from behind her. She whirled around and found the girl, dressed in a typical Chinese jacket and hat, ready to leave. "You bring money?"

"Yes," Lily said, absurd with relief. She held up the money. "If you give me wrong information, I will find you through this hotel. They will be *happy* to help me since you're running out without a word. Understand?"

She didn't want to threaten, but the right information was so important. Every second Melody was with those people was an eternity.

"I no give you wrong information. Xiao-lian is a good girl."

"Okay, Xiao-lian, tell me what you know."

ೞ ೲ

Ray tried not to panic. Lily had come in, looking like she'd been rolling in the hay with someone, took his money, then ran back out. Whatever she'd been doing, it wasn't getting their fucking breakfast.

Anger was building inside him along with something suspiciously like pain.

Trust me.

He dressed quickly and followed his wife downstairs. The urge overwhelmed him and he had to know what she was doing. When he reached the bottom of the stairs, he saw Lily exiting the kitchen and his stomach dropped to his feet. She looked like a slut.

The desk clerk waited for her with a leer. She tucked a piece of paper into her blouse and smiled at the idiot. He murmured and did his best to see down her cleavage. Ray's hands fisted and he barely controlled the rage coursing through him. He wanted to kill the son of a bitch. What the hell was Lily doing?

"Tomorrow then? What time?" the desk clerk said.

Lily ran her finger down his cheek. "How about two o'clock?"

When her fingers disappeared into the man's mouth, Ray growled and stepped toward them. Lily's eyes widened and she stepped away. The little shit who had been sucking on her fingers had the nerve to look scared.

"Ray, I thought you were sleeping."

"Obviously."

"Hey, she tried to get me to go in the back with her, mister, I swear," the weasel said.

Lily frowned at him and opened her mouth to speak.

"I don't really give a rat's ass who is doing what. Lily, are you with me or not?" He wanted to find Melody so badly, it burned the back of his throat.

She hurried toward him and took his arm. He promptly shrugged off her hand and clamped down on the raw pain ripping through his gut. They walked back upstairs single file and Ray focused on her ass swaying in front of him, wondering who'd had their hands on it in the past hour.

After she stepped into the hotel room, Ray slammed the door and locked it from the outside. Locking another faithless woman away. There was no way he was going to allow her to ruin his chances of finding Melody.

"Ray, what are you doing? Did you just lock me in?"

"I'm going to find my daughter, with or without your help. You obviously came here to flirt and play with other men. That ain't gonna happen, sweetheart. I'll be back for you later."

Ray ignored Lily's shouts as he stomped off down the hallway. He'd find the goddamn Barbary Coast and his daughter. Seemed that no one else in the damn town was interested in helping, including his wife.

CR ℘

Lily sat in the hotel room alone, wondering if Ray was ever coming back. She'd spent the last four hours wondering where the heck he was. Without a chance to explain her actions, she knew Ray thought the worst, especially given his history with faithless women. She held back the tears of frustration through force of will. Her nails were ragged and the floor had new grooves in it from her pacing. Where was Ray?

When a knock sounded at the door, a screech flew from her mouth. She clamped her lips shut and took a deep breath.

"Who is it?" she called.

"The cavalry."

Trevor!

"The door is locked from the outside, Trevor. Can you go back downstairs and get a spare key?"

"What?" His astonishment was plain.

"I can explain, just go get the key please." Lily wrung her hands, waiting the last five minutes for the key to sound in the tumblers. She threw open the door and was astonished to find not only Trevor, but Brett, Jack, Ethan, Noah and Tyler outside the door. She smiled and hugged every one of them while they rolled their eyes and patted her shoulder.

She ushered them into the little room, then realized they nearly filled it from wall to wall with all their bulk.

"Where's Ray?" asked Tyler with a scowl.

"I don't know. He left about four hours ago after locking me in. I got information about where Melody might be and we've only got a few hours to prepare."

Trevor looked at her wringing hands and then at his brothers, nephew and brother-in-law. "Why don't you all go down to the coast and see if you can find him? I'll stay here with Lily. Ethan, keep your eye on Noah."

Noah scowled, looking like his adopted father. "I'm not a kid, Uncle Ethan."

"Yeah, well you're not a man yet either, squirt. Just stick with Ethan."

"As long as I get to help." Noah's honest words made Lily's heart swell. The Malloy family was truly amazing.

"All right, let's go." Ethan herded everyone out with one last nod to Trevor.

Trevor turned his shrewd eyes on her and raised his brows. "You know I won't let you leave by yourself."

The urgency was nearly overwhelming. "I've got to, Trevor. She's going to be auctioned off tonight."

The color drained from his handsome face. "Auctioned?"

"Yes. There is this man Mr. Shen who deals in slaves, the younger the better. The information I have is that all new girls are auctioned through his business within days of arriving. There is a rumor that he has younger than usual girls this time. I know she's there, Trevor, and I have to stop them."

She didn't like the desperate tone to her voice, but it couldn't be helped. God knows why Ray chose to lock her in before she'd had a chance to explain, but Lily wasn't about to let the opportunity to rescue Melody pass by.

Lily decided Trevor would have to play his part. "You and I are going."

He held up his hands. "Oh no, I'm not going anywhere with you. Ray would kick my ass into next year."

"I don't care about your ass, Trevor Malloy. We're talking about Melody's life. Now we've got to get changed so we can get down there."

She started pulling off his coat.

"Changed?" he croaked.

Ignoring his protests, Lily got to work. Their deception had to be believable. Melody's life depended on it, and as soon as they walked in the door to Shen's, their lives did too.

CHAPTER SIXTEEN

Regina lay on the bed, watching Billy dress. He was such a muscular man, all hard lines and bulging muscles. Some of them bulged more than others. She cackled at her own joke. The shipment had been high quality, she still felt euphoric twelve hours after leaving the Blue Room.

"I'm taking the girl with me to Shen's auction," he said as he began buttoning his shirt.

"What?"

"There's an auction tonight. He promised us twenty-five percent of the take."

Regina blinked and tried to focus on what he was saying.

"I thought he would find a direct buyer."

Billy shrugged into his vest and fastened his gold pocket watch to it.

"This way is easier. She'll be on the block with a dozen others for slaves. We can get our money right away, then live like kings."

Regina didn't like the malice she glimpsed in his eyes. A shudder raked down her spine.

"We have enough money to live like kings already."

He shook his head. "The way you smoke it, it will be gone in three months. We need more."

"You waste money on those Chinese lotteries and those stupid gambling games."

He cut his eyes to hers and glared. "At least mine will bring in more money. Yours gets you high and allows strangers to fuck you until you can't walk."

"Nobody fucks me without my permission."

He grinned sardonically. "So when you were passed out yesterday and Jimmy Chen paid me ten bucks to fuck you, you gave him permission?"

Her stomach heaved and bile burned the back of her throat. He *sold* her to Jimmy Chen? That filthy, fat piece of shit?

"How dare you." As she struggled to her feet, the room tilted and she grabbed the wall to keep from falling.

"Oh, I'll dare a lot of things," he said as he straightened his jacket and smoothed the lapels. "I'm taking her with me tonight. You can either let me or you can die."

Regina felt a twinge of fear at the look in his eyes. "How much will we get?"

He chuckled and stroked his chin. "Probably at least a thousand."

A thousand was twenty-five percent?

Thinking about all that money made heat pool low and hot in her belly. She stared down at the prominent bulge in his trousers.

"Take a bath, Queenie. You stink. I'll be back later and you can show me all you learned in the Blue Room."

Billy scooped up the drugged girl from the cot in the corner and was out the door before Regina could say a word.

Not that she was going to. She did need a bath and all that money was enough to make her shudder with want. She flopped back down on the bed and her hands drifted to her nipples beneath the flimsy chemise. As they puckered beneath her questing fingers, Regina fantasized about having her own Blue Room in the mansion they would buy on Nob Hill.

CB EO

Trevor was annoyed, but Lily ignored him. She dressed him as her manservant, slicked his hair back with pomade, and darkened his face with make-up so he looked a little less like a Malloy. Lily used some powder to hide the wound on his hairline.

She slipped on an old dress of her mother's. It was a bright purple gauzy gown that slid down her body like water. Slippery and sexy, it showed quite a bit of her bosom. It was the most beautiful dress her mother had owned and for some reason, Lily had kept it all these years. Now she knew why—so she could rescue her stepdaughter.

Fixing a jaunty hat with a dark purple veil over her face, Lily let a few tendrils of hair drift down to hang near her cleavage. After she slipped on her nicest shoes, Lily fisted her hands to stop the trembling.

She had to be strong. She had to do her best to become Lil again.

When she came out of the room, she laughed at the expression on Trevor's face.

"Lily? Is that you? Holy shit!"

"Now, Mason," she corrected in a sultry British accent. "You know enough to call me mistress."

Now he nearly swallowed his tongue. "Yes, mistress," he choked out.

"Let us proceed. We do not want to be late for the auction."

"No, we don't want to be late," he repeated.

With a trembling step forward, Mistress Rose left with her manservant Mason to attend Mr. Shen's slave auction in Chinatown.

CR SO

After eight hours of a whole lot of nothing, Ray was desperate and frustrated. No one talked in this city, nothing worked, not money or intimidation or even begging. Something Ray had never done. He discovered though that he would do anything to find his daughter.

The one thing he did find out was that the Barbary Coast was useless during the day. Businesses seemed to be legitimate when daylight burned. He was forced to wait until nightfall to continue his search. What he really wanted to do was tear apart the city brick by brick until he found her.

God only knew what was happening to Melody or what that bitch did to her. Just the thought of it sent him into a rage so deep, he literally saw red. He needed to calm down, to think, to plan.

Ray was staring at his fourth glass of whiskey when a large hand clamped down his shoulder.

"What the hell are you doing?"

Expecting a fight, Ray turned to find Ethan, Brett, Jack, Noah and Tyler all looming over him.

"What you doing here?" he growled.

"Trying to help," Jack replied. "Lily sent us looking for you."

Ray scoffed. "Lily. You mean in between the men she's servicing at the hotel?"

Tyler looked about ready to hit him. "Before you locked her in your room, you idiot, she'd found information about Melody but you were too busy being an ass to listen."

"What information?" His heart started skipping beats as he waited for Tyler's response.

"Why did you lock her in?" asked Brett in his quiet way.

"I caught her stealing my money and almost fucking some guy at the hotel."

He never saw the fist coming, but he felt it—a hard hit with enough force to knock him to the floor. The saloon was suddenly silent as his brothers stared at him. Shit, even Noah had disappointment in his eyes.

"It's okay, folks," said Jack from above him. "This here's our big brother. We're just taking him home."

"Don't get any blood on my floor," chimed a voice from behind the bar.

Ray glared at his brothers and Tyler. "Who hit me?"

"I did," said Brett.

Ray could not have been more astonished. *Brett* hit him?

"You have an incredible, beautiful, intelligent wife, Ray. And as soon as she does something you don't know about, you paint her with the whore brush and kick her to the curb. She was looking for Melody and has information about where she is. Unfortunately her sorry-ass husband wouldn't listen and locked her in a room. She sent us to find you, God only knows why. I wish now we hadn't come."

That was probably more words than Ray had ever heard come out of Brett's mouth. Unfortunately everything he said was true.

"I'm sorry," Ray mumbled.

"Not as sorry as you'll be if you don't treat Lily right," Brett threatened.

Ray held up a hand and Tyler pulled him to his feet. The world swam out of focus for a moment.

"Coffee," he heard Tyler say.

Within moments, a hot cup of coffee was pushed into his hands and he was sitting on the stool again.

"Drink it," Tyler ordered. "Before Brett tries to pound you again. We need to get back to the hotel."

Finally Brett's words sank in. "Lily found information about Melody?"

"Yup, and you better pray we're not too late. You've wasted the entire goddamn day already."

Jack's ominous words sent a chill straight to his heart. He hoped his own morose stupidity wasn't going to cost him his daughter and his wife. He gulped the hot coffee with a wince, then stood.

"Let's go."

ೞ ೱ

Lil smiled behind her veil. "*Wan shang hao,*" she said to the large Chinese man at the door. "I am newly arrived and looking for, shall we say, a companion? Mason is just too…hairy and hard for me sometimes. I need a soft touch. You understand, don't you? I understand there are companions available here tonight."

"*Wo bu hui jiang ying yu.*"

Of course he didn't speak English. Why would he admit to that? The man was built like a house and apparently didn't know how to smile either.

"Who is this, Jimmy?"

The voice came from behind her. It sounded so much like Archie she had to fight the urge to run. Instead she turned her most charming smile on the man behind her.

Big like a bull, dark hair, bowler hat and fancy duds. He fit the description of Regina's companion perfectly.

"I am Mistress Rose," she said. "I heard there was…business to be conducted at Mr. Shen's this evening. I am looking to acquire a new companion."

The man's beady eyes raked her up and down and she posed for him, thrusting her ample cleavage out for his perusal. Anything to get inside.

"And this?" He hooked a thumb at Trevor.

"My manservant, Mason."

"He stays here. You can come in with me, love." He took her elbow and led her to the door.

She looked back at Trevor. "I won't be long, Mason. Wait there."

"Yes, mistress," he said through clenched teeth, his eyes shooting sparks at her.

"Who are you, kind sir?" she asked.

"Billy Black," he said.

"Sounds a bit like Black Bart. He's gone now, isn't he?"

Her companion grinned and she was reminded of a shark. With very sharp teeth.

"He is. I'm here now."

"I am lucky to have found you then," she murmured coyly.

He leered at her bosom while his hand drifted down to her behind. He caressed one hip and she smiled through her humiliation.

"When do the festivities begin?"

He brought her through a kitchen filled with Chinese people, then down a dark hallway. At the end of the hallway, he slid a door open and ushered her into a red room with a dozen people in it. Most women were veiled, like her, others were dressed in cheaply made sacks of broadcloth with gingham handkerchiefs thrown over their heads, tied beneath their chin, wearing shoes with two-inch heels. These young women, some probably no more than fourteen, stared down at the floor, awaiting their fates. They were slaves up for auction. The men were all dressed like Billy, in expensive suits, although most were Chinese. A sweet, sickly odor permeated the room. Opium and tobacco. She ground her teeth together in repressed fury. That Melody would have to endure this was enough to make even Lily turn violent.

"I am looking for someone quite young," she said. "Someone I can teach to please me."

Billy nodded. "How young?"

She tapped her finger against her lips. He followed the movement hungrily.

"No older than eight, but no younger than five. That age is perfect…to teach."

Billy licked his lips. "How much you willing to pay?"

She raised her brow. "This is an auction, is it not? I will bid as all the others do."

He ran his fingers down her arm. "I've got one for you," he whispered. "You don't have to bid neither. You and me, we'll do business together."

"You must think me a fool if I believe that. I can assure you, I'm not a fool." Her heart jammed in her throat as she played the disinterested card. She silently prayed he'd buy it. Lily turned to walk away when he caught her arm and reeled her back against him.

"No, I can see you're not a fool," he said as he began kissing her ear. She felt his arousal pressing against her hip and said a prayer to be strong.

"I tell you, I got one for you. She's five or six, half-white. She's healthy too."

Lily made a show of running her hands along his shoulders. "Why should I believe you?"

"She's in my carriage now in the back. I can show you her and then you and me..." His hand closed around her breast, "...we can do business."

Think of Melody. Think of Melody.

"If I am to believe you, I must take Mason with me. You understand, don't you, darling?"

He nodded. "You are a smart businesswoman, Miss Rose."

"That's Mistress Rose, Billy."

His nostrils flared. He knew what it meant and was even more aroused than before. His erection pushed against her hip and Lily clenched her teeth to avoid running from him.

"Shall we go?"

Within minutes, they were back outside. She crooked her finger at Trevor who followed behind her. She felt the waves of anger and frustration rolling off him.

When they reached the dark alley that smelled so badly it made her eyes water, she motioned for him to stay put. A black carriage stood in the weak light thrown by the rear door of the building. Billy jumped in and stepped out with a blanketed bundle in his arms. When he pulled the blanket back, Lily's heart leapt for joy.

It was Melody and she obviously hadn't been bathed or allowed to use the facilities in days. Lily clapped a hand over her nose against the stench.

"She smells, Billy. And she looks terrible. I don't think we're going to be able to do business."

It took everything she had to turn and start to walk away.

"Wait, Mistress Rose," he called. "She's healthy. We just had to, you know, keep her quiet. Just gave her a little bit in her milk. It ain't hurt her none. A bath and some clean clothes and she'll be good as new."

Lily looked again and wrinkled her nose. "I don't know…"

"You can have her for two thousand. That's half what you'll pay in Mr. Shen's."

Two thousand?

She wondered how they'd find so much money, it was a small fortune. She knew Ray brought some with him, she hoped it was enough. No matter what, she'd get the two thousand dollars. There was no other choice to make.

"That's four times the going rate for one of those slaves inside, Billy."

He frowned, absorbing her knowledge, and switched tactics. "Yes, but she's half-white, and she's even younger than them. That makes her special and worth four times as much. She's untried, of that I can be certain."

Lily's stomach heaved and rolled like the deck of a ship, she bit her lip to keep from showing Billy her dinner. With her heart pounding in her throat and tears stinging the back of her eyes, Lily knew she had to play this right or Melody was lost.

"You clean her up and bring her to me at midnight. Jackson and Dupont Street at the Globe Hotel. I'll have your money." Just saying it out loud made her knees weak. She wanted to snatch Melody and run like hell.

"Deal."

Lily walked back toward Trevor with a swing to her hips.

"Oh, and Mistress Rose?" Billy looked at her expectantly. "Afterwards, maybe we can…have fun?"

"Rest assured, Billy Black. You bring me that girl all cleaned up and you will have a night you'll never forget."

CHAPTER SEVENTEEN

Ray couldn't find Lily. He and Tyler searched for an hour and found nothing but the clothes she'd worn strewn about the room, along with some of Trevor's. That wasn't like her. Now he wasn't angry anymore, he was plumb worried sick.

His brothers, Noah and Tyler were out looking for her while he stayed at the hotel waiting. Waiting was not his strong suit—in fact, he hated it. And now that he had to worry about Lily and Melody, he felt like tearing the hell out of the furniture just to release his anger.

The door opened and Lily walked in dressed like a high-priced courtesan in a slinky purple dress. Behind her was Trevor looking like a slicked back fop.

His anger surged. "Where the hell have you been? And why are you dressed like a whore?"

Lily reared back as if he'd slapped her. Her face was drawn and pale and her lip trembled. Her eyes were pools of pain.

"I've been out finding Melody. Where have you been?" she asked, sticking her chin up in the air.

"I…I tried…" He cleared his throat as his heart pinched at the memory of exactly where he'd ended up. "I tried to find information, but I couldn't get anyone to talk to me. Somehow I ended up in a bar waiting for dark and my brothers dragged my sorry ass back here." He realized what Lily said and his heart leapt. "What do you mean finding Melody? Where is she?"

"I bought her."

Ray's mouth dropped open and he sank onto the bed. All the fear, the uncertainty and the anger swished around in his stomach like an acid cocktail. She *bought* her?

"Money hasn't changed hands yet. That's why we're here. We need two thousand dollars. Fast. We've got an hour and half."

Trevor finally closed the door and stared at Ray. Hard. Gone was the flirting, sassy-mouthed boy.

"Lily was amazing, Ray. She fooled all of them and brokered a deal to get her back. She even saw Melody. You've got no quarrel with her. But I'd like to knock your teeth out right about now."

His eyes were hard with anger. Ray looked inside at his own behavior and felt shame. She asked him to trust her and he hadn't. He had immediately thought the worst and let no one tell him any different. He'd gone off half-cocked and wasted nearly a day. A day Melody spent without him, alone and unprotected.

"I'm sorry," Ray offered pitifully. There was nothing he could do to make up for acting like such an ass.

"Don't apologize to me. Apologize to your wife. She's a goddess." With that, Trevor slammed into the hallway, leaving them alone. Lily's spine was straight and she gripped her reticule so hard, he was surprised it hadn't ripped in half.

"I'm sorry, Lily. I…I have a hard time trusting people and…"

She waved one gloved hand. "There isn't time for that now. Do you have two thousand dollars?"

He grimaced and shook his head. "I've got about twelve hundred."

"We need eight hundred more."

"I can do the math too."

"Stop it," she said, stepping forward to poke a finger into his chest. "Stop thinking about you and think about her. Ray, if you could have seen her…" She pulled the hat off her head and tossed it on the bed. "She was dirty and smelled like urine. And…and they drugged her. Oh, Jesus, they gave her opium."

Tears rolled down her face, smearing the make-up she had applied. He felt like crying too. His daughter was out there lying in her own filth with opium racing through her veins and he was sitting in a hotel room feeling sorry for himself.

"I'm sorry," he said, this time with a rasp to his voice he didn't bother to hide.

Ray clasped her trembling body to him tightly and rocked back and forth. He was more scared than he'd ever been in his life.

"We need to find my brothers and see if we can get the other eight hundred."

She nodded against his shoulder.

"I love you, Lily."

Lily's head snapped back and she looked at him with her mouth a small "O" of surprise. Her nose was red, as were her eyes, and her face splotchy, but she never looked more beautiful.

"I love you too, Ray."

He kissed her gently, then stood, anchoring her to his side.

"Let's go save our daughter."

CR ℘

Billy whistled as he carried the child back into the apartment. Regina lay on the bed, staring out through the window into the night.

"We need to clean her up."

She turned and looked at him. "Hmmmm?"

"I've got a private buyer. She insists on having the girl clean, so get your ass up and get water to wash her."

He set the girl on the bed next to Regina. She scuttled away like a cockroach until she stood, wrinkling her nose at the child.

"Wash her?"

"Are you deaf, bitch? We're going to make two thousand dollars on this sale. Wash her."

Regina nodded then went to the kitchen to get water.

Billy rubbed his hands together as he stared down at the two thousand dollar prize he'd taken for his own. Perhaps he'd take the money *and* the girl. Then fuck Mistress Rose until she couldn't scream any more.

He watched as Regina washed the child, slopping water and soap all over the bed. He didn't care as long as she was clean.

"Put her in one of your robes or something."

"But, Billy…"

"Shut up, Queenie, and do it."

With more grumbling, Regina went and retrieved her blue satin robe, wrapping the child in it. As she bent over her task, Billy decided he was done with Regina. She'd turned into a harpy just as all the others had done.

When she straightened, Billy calmly stood behind her, kissed the nape of her neck, then put both hands around it and snapped it.

Stepping over Regina's body, he picked up the girl and walked out the door.

CHAPTER EIGHTEEN

The Malloys all pooled their money together and had just over two thousand dollars. Ray gazed at the people surrounding him, realizing how lucky he was to have them. Their anxious faces and commitment to rescuing Melody was enough to make him almost tear up. Almost.

Lily put the money in her reticule, which she secured to her wrist. Pulling on her gloves, she looked at him and gave him a small smile.

"We should be back within an hour."

"Back? What do you mean back? I'm coming with you."

She shook her head. "This Billy Black is too smart for that. If I show up with more men, he'll run, I know it. Just Trevor, well Mason, and I must go. You stay here and wait."

"No."

"You have to trust me." Her eyes implored him.

"It's not you I don't trust. It's this man who kidnapped my daughter. Pardon me for feeling he's not worth the spit I can hurl at him."

"I won't risk Melody's life for your pride, Ray."

Was it pride? Was that what was urging him on? He knew he had an excess of it, but would he allow it to interfere with what he knew must be?

"It's hard, Lily. I...I feel like such a shitty father."

She cupped his cheek and her lavender scent wafted under his nose. He breathed in deeply, using the power of her to calm himself.

"You are an excellent father. The proof is in that little girl. She's smart, clever and a caring person. No parent ever did a better job, especially alone."

She kissed him, then ran her gloved thumb along his bottom lip. He inwardly shivered at the lust she ignited with such a simple touch.

"Can I wait a block away at least?"

She pursed her lips. "Three blocks."

"Two."

"Okay, two." She turned to Trevor who stood in the corner talking softly to Tyler, Noah and Brett. "Ready, Mason?" she asked in clipped British tones.

To Ray's astonishment, Lily changed in front of his eyes. When she walked, she swayed like a trained courtesan. Her entire demeanor became one of sex and pleasure. This was his mousy little governess?

"Of course, mistress," replied Trevor with a bow.

Together they walked out of the room and into danger. Ray scowled at the closed door, then glanced at the rest of his brothers and Tyler. Noah's eyes were as wide as saucers.

"I told her we'd wait two blocks away. Grab up those bags and anything else here. We're not coming back after we get Melody."

Tyler nodded. "Let's go."

☙ ❧

The inevitable fog from the water had drifted along the streets until it was difficult to see more than fifty yards away. Lily and Trevor sat in a hansom cab near the corner of the rendezvous point. She picked at her gloves, her stomach jumping like a bucket of frogs.

What if he didn't show up? What if he tried to take Melody and the money? What if he tried to kill them?

Too many what ifs. She'd drive herself crazy thinking about what could go wrong. She had to concentrate on staying in character and getting Melody back no matter what.

Trevor sat up abruptly from the corner where he slouched. "I hear something."

She did too. Horses hooves clattering along the street. They stopped nearby although the fog made it difficult to pinpoint anything.

"Go out and check to see if it's him."

"Why me?"

She rolled her eyes. "You are my manservant. You will always do what I tell you. Besides, that's what servants are for, to step into danger before his mistress."

He scowled. "Next time I get to be the master and you get to be the servant."

She tried to grin at his attempt at humor, but it fell short.

He kissed her cheek and stepped out of the carriage. She heard the murmur of men's voices, then footsteps coming back toward her carriage. The door opened suddenly and she bit her lip to stifle a shout.

Billy Black looked in at her with one raised eyebrow. "Did you bring the money?"

"Yes," she said with a sniff. "Did you clean up the child? I must see that she is clean and healthy before I give you one cent."

"Sure thing, love. Step out and we'll do business."

Lily couldn't see Trevor, but she really had no choice. She held out her hand and stepped down from the carriage onto the sidewalk slick with fog.

"Well, where is she? I've got another engagement in an hour, Mr. Black. I cannot dally here with you."

"Of course, Mistress Rose. Step right this way to my carriage and we'll have a look." His oily voice sent spiders of disgust skittering down her skin.

"No one will come looking for this one, will they?" she asked.

"Not a chance. She isn't from around here. Besides her mother's dead."

Dead? Did that mean he killed Regina?

They walked over to his black carriage with his meaty hand clamped to her elbow. She glanced down at his hand then up at his face, half hidden in the shadows thrown by the street lamp.

"I do not need assistance walking, Mr. Black. Take your hand off my elbow or I will take it off. This rose has thorns. Sharp ones."

He laughed. "Feisty one, aren't you? What are you going to do, bite it off with your sharp, little teeth?"

She smiled with enough hate to light up the entire city. "I'll let it be a surprise. Now, remove your hand."

Something in her tone must have told him she meant business because he removed his hand. She was startled to see Trevor sitting on the sidewalk holding the side of his head. A thread of panic wound around her, but she held it back, opting to sound annoyed instead.

"What did you do to Mason?" she asked impatiently. "I do need him. What will I do without my manservant? I can't be expected to serve myself."

Billy's gaze raked her up and down slowly. "I don't expect you ever need to serve yourself. Too many bucks waiting in line to do it for you."

She sniffed disdainfully. "It's an exclusive line. One by invitation only."

Billy paused with his hand on the carriage door handle. "You inviting me?"

She raised one eyebrow and made an impatient gesture with her hand. "Mr. Black, if I didn't know any better, I would swear you don't want to do business with me. In another minute, I will find another seller or go back to Mr. Shen's."

"No need to get snippy," he said defensively. "Here, have a look."

He reached in and scooped up a bundle from the bottom of the carriage. The bastard put that child on the floor. He had her in a different blanket, wearing a large women's satin robe. Lily leaned forward and peered at the little girl, trusting the darkness to hide the relief and joy at seeing Melody.

"She definitely smells better." Lily felt Melody's arm. "She's skinny."

Billy shrugged. "She's strong though, I swear to you. Do you want her or not?"

Lily pursed her lips together and looked unconvinced. She glanced at Trevor.

"Oh, do get up, Mason. Come help me decide. Do you think this one will be better than the others? They all disappointed me. I don't want that to happen again."

Billy grinned, his teeth feral in his face. "She won't disappoint, I guarantee it."

Trevor staggered to his feet, the side of his face wet with blood. He peeped at the girl in Billy's arms.

"Scrawny, mistress. I don't know if she's the one." Trevor choked out his lines like a true thespian. Lily just hoped Billy would believe their act.

"You're right. But I think I like her." She turned to Billy. "Fifteen hundred."

Lily's heart hammered in her throat and she prayed to every God she could think of that her ploy worked. She had to negotiate or Billy might become suspicious.

"You are a businesswoman, Mistress Rose. I appreciate that. Fine then, I'll let her go for fifteen hundred, not a penny less. But I keep the robe."

"The robe?"

"Yes." Billy's smile grew wider. "That robe cost me at least fifty. I want it back."

Lily struggled not to let her disgust show. "Fine, you can have the robe back. I have clothing that will fit her. Most of it is pink as little girls should wear."

She handed her reticule to Trevor. "Count out the money, Mason, while Mr. Black deposits our purchase in the carriage."

Billy brought Melody to the carriage and laid her on the seat. With a grunt, he pulled the robe off and flopped the blanket over the unconscious child. Lily pretended to be interested in the storefront beside them.

"I do like that hat. I must come back when they're open, Mason. Do remind me."

Trevor handed her the money. She in turn handed it to Billy, who snatched the money and counted it quickly.

"You know I could take you and the girl."

She narrowed her eyes and shook her head. "The three men hiding in the shadows wouldn't stand a chance against the five men behind them."

Billy threw back his head and laughed like he had never heard anything as funny as someone threatening his life.

"Like I said, a businesswoman, a clever one. I should take you," Billy threatened.

Lily whipped out the derringer from her sleeve and pointed it directly at Billy's black heart.

"Not unless you fancy a new hole in your pretty clothes, Mr. Black."

He held up his hands, the robe dangling from one of them. "Okay, then, no need to get disagreeable."

"On your way then," she said as she gestured with the gun toward his carriage. "Nice doing business with you."

He smiled and Lily glimpsed the man he could have been beneath the evilness that had taken over his life. "Sure you won't change your mind and come with me?"

Lily tapped her cheek with one gloved finger as she pretended to contemplate his offer.

"No, I prefer my autonomy, Mr. Black. Thank you all the same."

Lily stepped into the carriage and Trevor closed the door behind her. He climbed into the driver's seat with a creak and within moments, the carriage was rolling.

Lily shook so hard, her teeth knocked together. She reached out and gathered Melody into her arms, the warm body penetrating the chill in her soul. She cried softly as she crooned to her daughter.

Five minutes later, the carriage stopped and the door flew open. Ray came rushing in and then looked behind him.

"Finish up then meet us at the train station," he told the others.

He slammed the door and sat across from her. The fear and naked anguish in his eyes were staggering. She set Melody into his arms.

"She's unconscious. I think they gave her laudanum or perhaps opium in her milk. I think she'll wake up by morning."

"She's okay though?"

"She seems to be just fine. Thin and pale, but okay."

"Ah, God, little note. Oh, my sweet baby," he said in a hoarse whisper.

He slowly closed his eyes and his arms. Silent sobs shook him as he hugged his daughter close. Lily looked out the window to give him a small modicum of privacy. To be so loved by your parents. Her children, including Melody, would always know that from her.

Without love, there was only emptiness. Love filled up your arms, your heart and your life.

CHAPTER NINETEEN

Lily changed in the carriage. She carefully removed her mother's dress and folded it neatly, then placed it and her father's derringer together in the bottom of her bag. Funny how in life her parents tried their best, but failed. But in death, a piece of each of them allowed her to succeed in saving her new daughter's life…and her husband's heart.

She slipped on her grey wool traveling dress. She smiled when she remembered she'd been wearing it when she first met Ray.

"Are you sure we're not being followed?" she asked as she buttoned up the front.

Ray didn't look up from Melody. "Tyler's sure there were only three of them, and they're taken care of. I think we can take his word for it. He was a bounty hunter for nearly ten years."

Lily nodded, still too worked up to relax.

"Thank you," he whispered.

When she looked into his eyes, she saw her future, her past and her present together. He showed her everything, *everything*. She'd never felt so blessed in her life.

"I'd do anything for her or you, Ray. I'm just so glad it all worked out."

He grimaced. "Next time you shouldn't have to do the dirty work."

"I didn't mind. At least my childhood brought me something I could use to help her. A little Chinese and some street smarts, and a whole lot of luck."

"How long do you think she'll be out?"

Lily shrugged. She took out a dress and underthings to dress Melody with.

"Hard to say. Hopefully no more than a day."

"A day?" he shouted.

She frowned. "Do you think to scare her awake? No need to shout, Ray. I'm right in front of you."

"Sorry," he mumbled.

She covered his hand with hers. "No reason to be. Now let's get this little girl in some clothes before she catches a cold."

Together they dressed her in warm clothing and in no time, they arrived at the train station.

They traveled separately so as not to seem like a large, memorable group. Ray, Lily and Melody huddled on a bench until morning. The rest of their group kept watch from various corners of the station and out on the platform. Everyone was quiet and withdrawn, waiting for Melody to wake up.

Lily purchased a basket of muffins and milk to take on the train with them for when Melody did wake. It seemed like days before they could board the eastbound train first thing in the morning. Ray's parents wired money through Western Union to pay for a private compartment.

The sun rose as the train chugged along and still Melody slept on. Lily kept checking her for signs of an overdose, but she appeared to be fine. That bastard Billy must have given her an elephant's dose to make her sleep so long. A sudden thought struck her.

"Do I want to know what happened to Billy?" Lily blurted.

Ray's grin was wolfish. "No, you probably don't. He won't be kidnapping little girls anymore."

"Was anyone else hurt?" Lily was worried about her new family.

"No, the boys are all fine. Apparently even Noah showed what he was made of."

Lily didn't ask any more questions after that. She figured it was better if she kept her knowledge to a minimum. The Malloys were a family that protected their own, even if they flayed each others' hides to do it.

Mid-morning brought pacing and short tempers. Lily had to break up two fights and countless arguments. Sending them off in different directions, she locked everyone out of the compartment except Ray. He wouldn't let go of his daughter. He sat and stared at her, touching her hair, kissing her forehead and rocking her.

"I think Regina is dead," Lily said.

Ray's gaze snapped to hers. "What makes you say that?"

She shrugged. "A feeling I got from Billy. He told me her mother was dead."

He snorted. "What goes around comes around."

"She must have been nice once," Lily offered.

"She was manipulative, selfish and greedy. And I don't want to talk about her. If she isn't dead, and she ever comes around my daughter—"

"Our daughter," Lily corrected.

"Our daughter again, I will kill her."

Lily gazed out the window at the passing scenery. Who would have thought two months ago she would have traveled by train from one side of the country to the other? Most people never get the chance. The mountains of California gave way to the dry flatlands of Nevada.

"Sing."

"Sing?" Lily asked.

"Yes, words and music together, do you remember how? Melody loved to hear you sing." He looked up at her with haunted eyes. "Please."

Lily leaned forward and kissed him. "Of course."

She started to sing her favorite hymn, "Amazing Grace". She felt as if she'd been saved when she stepped off the train in Cheshire, Wyoming. Saved from a life of loneliness and what ifs.

During the second verse, Ray hummed along with her.

Lily sang until her throat was too sore to sing any more. She sounded more like a rusty wheel than anything. Ray handed her the jar of milk. She took it gratefully and twisted the cap off. As she swallowed a greedy gulp, a little voice piped up.

"Why did you quit singing, Mama?"

Lily nearly dropped the milk in her lap as Ray stared at Melody in astonishment. Her dark eyes were open and clear.

With a loud whoop, Ray squeezed her tightly.

"Pa, you're squishing me again. Cut it out!" She pushed at his big chest with her little hands.

Lily set the milk down and dropped to her knees in front of them. She reached out and touched Melody's cheek.

"Is it okay if I call you Mama?" she asked.

Lily nodded. "It's more than okay. I would like nothing better."

Ray put Melody on one knee and pulled Lily up beside him. They wrapped their arms around each other and held on. Lily finally felt that persistent hole in her heart close completely.

CR ∞

Ray must have telegraphed his family. By the time the train slid into Cheshire, there must have been fifteen or twenty people waiting for them. With a mighty cheer, Melody was passed from aunt to uncle to grandpa to grandma to cousin. Kisses, hugs and squeals echoed in the cold air.

Ray stood with his arm around Lily, watching his daughter get showered with love. He turned to Lily and smiled.

She didn't see it often, but when she did, it about knocked her bloomers clean off. Raymond Malloy was a devastatingly handsome man. And he was all hers.

"What are you thinking?" Lily asked.

"How a governess from New York turned my life upside down."

"Oh, sorry," she said, pulling from him.

He yanked her back against his chest, his fingers grazing under her breast. Her breath hitched as a curl of heat snaked through her.

"You're not going anywhere, Mrs. Malloy. We've got a honeymoon to get to."

In front of everyone, he swooped in to give her a heart-stopping kiss. His tongue swiped inside her mouth until she was delirious with want and hunger. She clenched at his shoulders, afraid she'd fall on her fanny.

When he finally released her, she realized his family had walked away to the wagons and horses waiting beyond the platform. Melvin stood near the station door; he gave a small wave and went back inside.

She glanced up at her husband. He touched her cheek with one gloved finger.

"I love you, Lily."

She smiled and squeezed his hand. "I love you too, Ray. Ready to go home?"

"Yes, let's go home."

Ray's parents tucked Melody safely into the back of their carriage with mounds of blankets. Francesca climbed in with her and held on tight. She shooed away Lily's efforts to join them.

"Stay with your husband, Lily. He needs you. We'll bring Melody home," Francesca said.

After everyone left in the wagons and carriages, the only mode of transportation left was a horse. A large gray horse that made Lily's stomach clench.

"I guess we ride Shadow home." Ray led her down the platform stairs.

Lily tried to force away the panic that crept down her spine, but it didn't work. Ray must have felt her tug on his hand. He looked back at her with a frown. "What's wrong?"

"Isn't there a carriage or a wagon we can use?" She hated the fact her voice trembled.

Ray scooped her up in his arms and she squealed at the sudden change in altitude. "What are you doing?"

"Showing you that Shadow is nothing to be afraid of. Hold on." He practically threw her on top of the large beast. Lily screeched and tried to clamber down, but he held her in place with one big hand while he mounted behind her.

The horse picked that moment to whicker and move beneath her. Lily's stomach rolled to the right.

"Oh my God, Ray. I can't do this."

His arms surrounded her and tucked her close to him. The warmth of his body had little effect on the cold panic gripping her. The muffin she'd eaten on the train threatened to make a reappearance.

"Trust me, sunshine," Ray whispered in her ear as he kneed the horse into motion.

Lily screeched again and gripped the saddle horn like a lifeline. "Stop, please, Ray."

He pulled the horse to a halt, then turned her face to look at him. "I won't let anything hurt you. Please trust me. I want to help you."

The sincerity in his eyes spoke to her heart. "I'll try, j-just go really slow, okay?"

He grinned and kissed her softly. "That's Mrs. Malloy talking."

Lily's chest puffed with pride at the compliment. One had to be tough to be a Malloy. She was determined to live up to the name.

"Are you ready?" he asked.

Lily nodded and he took her hands in his. "Hold the reins with me so you can see how to control him."

With patience she never expected, Ray taught her how to ride a horse. Ten minutes passed without a panic attack or a smidge of nausea. Lily pronounced herself ready for the ride home.

"It's going to take us at least two hours. Are you sure you're ready?" Ray sounded so concerned it made Lily smile.

"I'm ready, Mr. Malloy. Let's ride!"

He kneed Shadow into motion and the trot became a gallop. The cold wind and the warm sunshine battled over them as they rode together. By the time they were halfway home, Lily wondered how she could have ever been afraid of horses. Shadow's gait was smooth and with Ray's arms around her, she felt safe and secure.

When the ranch house came into view, Lily's heart beat faster and tears pricked her eyes. *Home.* A place she never even thought to have. Now she had a home, a husband and a daughter. Lily's life had taken an amazing turn in the last two months.

"Is Melody here?" Lily wondered if Ray's parents had brought her.

"No, Mama and Papa are keeping her at their ranch tonight so we can be alone for once."

Ray's husky words sent a shiver down her spine. Alone with her husband, a true wedding night. The possibilities seemed endless, the pleasure boundless.

He pulled the horse to a stop and dismounted. Lily couldn't contain the dance of excitement in her belly. As he reached up and helped her down, his lips locked onto hers. As their tongues tangled and bodies heated, he carried her into the house, dangling in front of him, her breasts pressed tightly against his chest.

She vaguely heard a grunt and a chuckle, but the door closed behind them too quickly for her to determine if it was Rafe or Clyde. It didn't matter, they'd take care of the horse and steer clear of the house for the rest of the day.

The purple and orange rays of sunset shone through the windows of the bedroom. Ray set her on her feet and cupped her face in his hands.

"I can't believe you're really mine, you're really here to stay."

"Believe it," Lily whispered then kissed his palm. "You aren't getting rid of me anytime soon."

"Thank God."

Ray removed her clothes, kissing and caressing the exposed skin. Goose bumps danced across her body as her heart beat for her husband, her lover, her soul. He shucked his clothes quickly, then stood in front of her, nude and aroused.

"You're incredible, sunshine."

The sincerity in his voice stole her breath. He cupped her breasts and rubbed his thumbs across her nipples, sending shockwaves straight to her throbbing pussy. When his mouth closed on one, she pressed her thighs together to ease the ache. As his tongue laved and teased her, she caressed his shoulders, feeling the smooth skin, the hard muscles.

Ray dropped to his knees and buried his face in her belly, holding her tight. "I love you."

Lily ran her fingers through his soft sunset-touched hair. "I love you too, Ray."

"I never thought I'd say that to another woman."

"I know and it means everything to me." She pulled him up until he stood. "*Everything*."

Lily swore she saw a tear in one eye, but before she could ask, he had her on the bed and lay on top of her. His hard, hairy chest pushed against hers, tickling and tantalizing her nipples.

"You feel so good."

"Mmmm, so do you," he groaned as he trailed kisses along her jaw to her ear. Nibbles and licks sent shivers down clear to her toes. His cock nudged between her legs and she spread them wide in invitation. She felt hungry and only Ray could satisfy her.

The frantic beating of her heart mirrored his. It was time, past time. They needed to make love, to heal and be healed.

"Please, Ray," Lily nearly begged him. She clawed at his back as he continued to gently tease her. "I can't wait. Please."

Ray seemed to understand her urgency because he stopped teasing and slid into her in one thrust. Lily gasped as he filled her completely. Time stood still and shrank down to two hearts beating as one. He rested his forehead on hers and their breaths mingled.

Ray shook above her and Lily wrapped her arms around him as far as they'd go. She hung on, giving him everything in her heart as his body joined with hers. She clenched around his hardness and he groaned in a gust.

"Jesus, Lily, I…I'm holding on by a thread."

She stroked the skin on his shoulders and wiggled beneath him. "Why are you holding on? Let go and ride, my love, let's ride."

He shuddered and opened his eyes. Inches apart, he looked into hers and showed her his soul.

"You healed me, sunshine."

Her heart hitched and a tear rolled down her cheek. She kissed him, licking and nibbling until he finally opened his mouth. Their tongues began to dance along with their bodies, sliding heat and passion. He rolled over and suddenly Lily found herself astride him.

Her fingers caressed his chest, lightly scraping his nipples. He groaned and pushed up into her. Lily, no longer afraid of reaching for anything, started riding her husband. Up and down, slowly then quickly, she pleasured herself and him. He grasped one breast and held on tight, forcing her to only move an inch at a time. Sweet torture.

"Don't come yet," he whispered against her skin.

"Ray, I can't… Help me." She was ready to explode, to reach for the heavens that beckoned so close.

He cupped her neck and fused his mouth with hers as he thrust into her deeply. The pleasure exploded over them, raining a torrent of ecstasy that soaked them. Lily's tears blended with Ray's as her body shook with the force of their love.

It seemed like an eternity until she caught her breath and collapsed on top of him. He ran his hand down her skin, sliding in the slickness of their passion.

"That was…" He flipped her over and propped himself on his elbows to look into her eyes. "Incredible."

Lily couldn't stop the wide smile from spreading across her face. After their first kiss on the floor of the kitchen, he'd called it incredible. This…this was even more.

This was forever.

BETH WILLIAMSON

You can't say cowboys without thinking of Beth Williamson. She likes 'em hard, tall and packing. Read her work and discover for yourself how hot and dangerous a cowboy can be.

Beth lives just outside of Raleigh, North Carolina, with her husband and two sons. Born and raised in New York, she holds a B.F.A. in writing from New York University. She spends her days as a technical writer, and her nights immersed in writing hot romances for her readers.

To learn more about Beth Williamson, please visit www.bethwilliamson.com. Send an email to Beth at beth@bethwilliamson.com, join her Yahoo! Group, http://groups.yahoo.com/group/cowboylovers, or sign up for Beth's monthly newsletter, Sexy Spurs, http://www.crocodesigns.com/cgi-bin/dada/mail.cgi/list/spurs/.

The Malloy Family series continues when honey-tongued devil
Trevor Malloy meets his match in saloon owner Adelaide Burns

The Gift

(c) 2006 Beth Williamson

Available in ebook November 21, 2006 at Samhain Publishing.

Adelaide Burns has owned the Last Chance Saloon since her father died and left it to her two years earlier. A tougher, more street-wise redhead couldn't be found west of the Mississippi.

Trevor Malloy loves women, in all shapes and sizes. He's spent most of his adult life chasing anything in a skirt. He thinks he can charm Adelaide just as easily as every other woman.

Boy, is he dead wrong.

Enjoy this excerpt from

Trevor stopped his horse on the outskirts of the main street in Cheyenne. Busy, but not bustling busy, exactly where he wanted to start his new career. Two saloons sat on either side of him. One was the Silver Spittoon, the other the Last Chance. He surveyed the horseflesh tied up outside and determined the Last Chance had better clientele.

A small hotel sat next door, convenient for his purposes. He tied up the gelding then headed to the hotel to check in. Trevor wasn't stupid enough to walk into a saloon with every cent he owned in his pocket. God only knew what kind of cheaters he'd find within its walls. Sometimes even the dealers cheated.

With his saddlebags slung over one shoulder, he stepped into the hotel to make arrangements for a room. The clerk insisted on being paid up front.

Trevor planned on only staying a week—long enough to make money to fund the rest of his trip to Texas. He counted out fourteen dollars and handed it to the bespectacled clerk.

"I expect a hot bath every day and at least one hot meal included for that price."

"Yes, sir, that's included. The water might still be warm upstairs if'n you want a bath now." He pointed toward the stairs and handed Trevor a key.

Trevor thanked the clerk and headed upstairs to his room. A bath sounded pretty good, but he really wanted to get acquainted with the saloons and the poker action. He made sure there were no bugs in his bed before dropping his gear off. Nothing like scratching the night away in someone else's mess. He was pleasantly surprised to find the hotel was clean—they must be going after all the travelers coming in on the railroad now that service was picking up.

Trevor emerged into the evening air and took a deep breath. It smelled like success. Sweet and pungent. With a chuckle, he headed into the Last Chance Saloon.

The saloon didn't have any dancing girls, but there were definitely nicely shaped gals serving. He winked at two of them while sauntering toward the bar—they both giggled and winked back. Good sign. The bar itself wasn't new, but it was well taken care off with brass rails top and bottom, and stools that had held more than a few asses. The bartender was a big man with a handlebar mustache and a glare that could curdle milk.

Trevor smiled and headed for the bar, trying to keep his eyes averted from the tables toward the back where the poker action was. No music played and there was an air of relaxed camaraderie in the saloon. That was also good news. Happy people played poker with better attitudes and there was less chance of a sore loser. Especially one with a gun.

"Evenin,'" Trevor said as he sat. "Beer please."

The bartender stared at him hard before nodding and setting a mug of beer down. "Four bits."

Steep price for beer, but Trevor set his money down and thanked the grumpy bartender. With one last glare, the man went back to his chore of wiping glasses. Trying not to look like he was spying, Trevor slowly turned and faced the saloon.

There were six tables, two of which had poker games in play. Six people sat at each of the poker tables, including two dealers, one of which was an incredibly curvy redhead with tits that literally made his mouth water.

Very interesting. A female dealer with hands as fast as greased lightning. She obviously was taught by someone with skills. Trevor had never seen a dealer quite like her before and his dick certainly appreciated her as well. Pouty full lips, framed by a pixie nose, freckle splashed complexion, incredible sunset red hair and eyes that looked sharper than his knife.

She glanced his way and then turned back to the table without so much as a twitch. Trevor wasn't sure if he should be insulted or not. He wasn't vain by any means, but most women looked at him twice. He'd been blessed with the best looks of the Malloy brothers, which was a fact he accepted at the age of ten when Mary Lou Harris kissed him behind the barn. That's when he realized his looks could bring him untold gifts from women, and not the kind you could necessarily buy.

Trevor sipped his beer and watched the poker game as closely as he could without appearing like he was watching. He wanted to play a hand or two that evening, and there was no need to look anxious. Casual interest, casual game. That was the ticket.

Now all he needed to do was charm the lady dealer and he had it made.

ભ ભ ભ

The stranger was, quite simply, stunning. Adelaide noticed him immediately and felt a hard kick of appreciation for his appearance. With wavy reddish brown hair and a smile that could melt butter, he sat at the bar and watched, pretending that he wasn't watching.

Adelaide spotted poker players within a minute—this one should have had gambler written on his forehead in grease pencil. Other than his looks, she didn't notice any other redeeming qualities. Gamblers had them in short supply.

When Parker and Curtis left for supper, the stranger stood, stretched, then picked up his beer and ambled over to the table. A long-legged gait, easy movements showing he was comfortable in his skin. With a devastating grin, he gestured to the open chair across from her.

"May I?"

Oh, Lord have mercy. His deep timbered voice sent skitters down her skin and made her nipples tighten like bowstrings. Adelaide had a brief moment of imagining that voice whispering in her ear before she squelched it and sent it packing. She'd sworn off handsome, smooth-talking men a long time ago, so this one didn't stand a chance in hell of getting into her bed, much less her heart.

"Chair's open if you're wanting to play, stranger. One dollar ante, five card draw, wild cards are dealer's choice. You in?" She kept shuffling the deck to maintain focus on what she was doing. His looks were distracting.

"Thank you kindly, pretty lady."

Well, that doused her unusual arousal, not completely, but a lot. She hated nonsensical shit like that. What was the point of that compliment? Did he honestly think she'd be so flattered she'd forget how to deal cards? Just put another fool trying the "I'm so handsome, won't you fall into my arms" routine she'd heard so many times.

"No thanks required, just the money. Five card draw, threes and sixes are wild. Ante up, fellas."

With four players left, the cards moved more quickly. Adelaide kept her eyes trained on the flirtatious stranger and his charming self. She damn well tried not to look at his long-fingered hands, at the way he held the cards, and caressed the edges. She just knew those fingers had an enormous amount of talent for things other than playing cards.

Focus, Addie. Don't let 'em distract you. Remember, you hold the cards.

Her grandfather's voice echoed in her ear. He'd taught her everything she knew about cards, and about life. She'd always followed his advice and it never steered her wrong.

Everyone took three cards, except Handsome. He took only one, with a wink, no less. Adelaide cocked one eyebrow and smirked. She received a chuckle in response.

"I can't help myself. Every time I see a pretty lady, I just lose my head," he said as he met the raise and smiled those pearly whites again.

"I might lose my supper if you're not careful." Adelaide finally looked at her cards when she realized the bet was to her. "See your five, raise you five."

"What's your name, darlin'?"

She'd give him his druthers; he didn't give up easily, did he? "You may call me Miss Adelaide."

"Mmmm, Addie...that fits perfectly. I'm Trevor Malloy."

"You're holding up the game, Trevor Malloy. See the bet or fold." Adelaide refused to give into the stranger's charms.

With another chuckle, Trevor saw the bet and called. She wasn't surprised to find he had three tens in his hand and took the pot. The gambling cowboy definitely knew what he was doing. Too bad he had no idea who he was playing against.

Adelaide hated to lose, no ifs, ands or buts. Especially to someone she didn't respect like silver-tongued cowboys. She was done playing—it was time to show sweet cheeks what a real gambler could do.

As things heat up between the Blacksmith's apprentice and the woman he dares not love, an element stronger than the both of them will test their limits, and the very foundation the town was built on.

Melting Iron
(c) 2006 Ann Cory

Available in ebook and print from www.samhainpublishing.com.

A lonely wife of a Blacksmith finds a spark of life in the young apprentice, Daniel. Stuck in a loveless marriage Evelynn dreams of a different life, away from her cold-hearted husband and his cruel ways. As her feelings grow for Daniel, she becomes restless and wonders what it would be like to have his tender hands on her naked flesh.

While things heat up between Daniel and Evelynn a relentless storm brews around Johnstown and rumors circulate that the dam is too weak to hold up against a heavy rain. As the water rises, Evelynn and Daniel are separated. Many lives are lost. Is their love strong enough to break free of Mother Nature's stronghold?

Warning: Contains explicit sexual situations and some violence.

Enjoy this excerpt from

The softness of his hands surprised her. Each touch radiated enough heat to melt the coldness from around her heart. She couldn't remember it ever being this way. No man, not even her husband, had ever caressed her flesh with such intended passion.

"You want me, don't you?"

She stared at his mouth. Firm, full, supple lips. They breathed new life into her with each fervent kiss. Was it wrong to want another man when she was married? Instincts told her the answer was clear. She was an adult, not a child. Of course it was wrong.

Still, the word infidelity played at her. It sparked mixed emotions, almost like a dare. It was forbidden. Disrespectful even. Why would she consider it?

He was excruciatingly close, making her body ache.

"What stops you from saying yes?"

His question was a double-edged sword. He knew, as well as she did, what the consequences were. Why was he baiting her? Evelynn shook her head. No. The question was why was she letting him?

As if in answer she held out her hand, her fingers pointing downward. The dim light of the lantern brought out the fine lines across her skin.

He jutted out his chin and looked hard into her eyes. "I am well aware of the piece of jewelry branded around your finger. Tell me, because I'm eager to hear, what does the ring signify for you?"

Eveylnn parted her lips to speak, but nothing came out. She wasn't ready for serious questions. With a dismissive shrug, she glanced off to the far corner of the barn.

"It means I have someone to answer to." She looked back at him, their eyes locked in a challenging gaze.

"And do you answer to him?"

Evelynn narrowed her eyes. "Not in the way you are suggesting."

His brows arched and he crossed his arms. "No? Please. Enlighten me."

Every nerve in her body was on edge.

She fixed her fists on her hips and tried to summon up a little attitude.

"What I mean is, I don't do whatever he commands. I am my own person, and I intend to remain unchanged. He may have given me a ring and a new last name, but he hasn't stripped me of my identity."

There. She'd said the words. The problem was they weren't at all true.

"No man ever should take away your identity."

Her body shook as she realized how close he now stood. "Wh-what?"

"No man should ever make a woman change or take away her self worth."

Evelynn snorted. He was just a young man, what did he know? "It's not as simple as you make it out to be. When two people live under the same roof for a long time, under the binding laws of marriage, they change. You give up certain things for one another."

"I see. In other words they strike a compromise. They find ways to be equals in the household. Am I getting warmer?"

She bit her lip. His presence warmed her entire being. Damn him and his desirable body. There was no way she was going to win here. Not with him less than a foot away, spouting the ideas of what marriage should be like, knowing full well they weren't the same as her ideals. Her tight fists strained her wrists.

"I don't want to talk about this anymore. Anything I say you are going to find something to argue about. I should go."

He reached out, catching a tuft of fabric from her dress. "I'm not trying to argue with you. I only want to understand. I had hoped you would stay a while longer."

His smile made it clear he would do whatever it took to sway her decision. He moved toward her, closing the distance to the point she could smell the soot in his hair.

"When I look into your beautiful green eyes, I see a tremendous amount of sadness. It will destroy you, if it hasn't all ready. I see a precious life not being lived to its fullest. You, my dear sweet Evelynn, aren't some item to be used and discarded on a daily basis. In the time I've lived here, I have never seen your husband look at you with the same kind of excitement I feel coursing through my veins. I've never even witnessed him touch you with a gentle hand."

She puffed out her chest and put her hands on her hips. "And I suppose you can see through walls?"

He pressed his finger to her lips and shook his head. The feel of his skin sent her mind into a flurry of confusion.

"It breaks my heart to think you have resigned yourself to this dismal way of life. There is a burst of energy inside you waiting to get out. I can see it!"

She laughed nervously and wanted to turn away, but he wouldn't let her gaze falter.

"You deserve to be loved. I want you to know how it feels to have someone think about you from the moment they wake, until the time they fall asleep, and for every second in between. Let me find a way to put hope into your heart and fire in your belly."

Shivers crept along her skin as his lips sought out the curvature of her neck – the sweet spot – where the blend of pleasurable and painful tickles drew the very warmth from between her thighs.

He watched her. "Would you deny these very things? Can you honestly say you don't want me?"

Her lower lip trembled. Where was her voice when she needed it most?

Daniel's lips brushed against her earlobe, his voice deep and sensuous. "Tell me. I need to hear the words from you. If you want me to leave you alone from now on, I will. But I have to hear it."

Samhain Publishing, Ltd.

It's all about the story…

Action/Adventure
Fantasy
Historical
Horror
Mainstream
Mystery/Suspense
Non-Fiction
Paranormal
Red Hots!
Romance
Science Fiction
Western
Young Adult

http://www.samhainpublishing.com